The Silence of Seabrook

Eric Brown

BROWN FAMILY BOOKS

Printed in the United States of America
ISBN 979-8-9952552-3-9 (paperback)
ISBN 979-8-9952552-4-6 (hardcover)

Interior design: Eric Brown
Cover design by Eric Brown
First Edition: 2026

For my daughters,
who inspire every story I write.

Chapter 1

Winter changed Seabrook in ways tourists never saw. In summer the harbor felt busy and bright, the docks crowded with boats and voices and the sharp smell of diesel drifting over the water. Shops stayed open late. People laughed easily. Even the gulls sounded different, their cries sharp and impatient as they fought over scraps along the marina railings. But winter stripped the place down to something quieter.

The fishing boats remained, rocking slowly against their lines, but most of the charter vessels were gone. Their slips sat empty, ropes tied neatly around cleats that would not see use again until spring. The air carried the heavy smell of salt and wet wood, mixed with the distant iron scent of the Pacific pushing steadily against the coast.

Jonah Harris stood at the edge of Dock C with his hands buried deep in the pockets of his jacket. A low gray sky pressed down over the harbor. The clouds had been sitting there all morning, thick and unmoving, the kind that held rain but never quite released it. The wind off the water carried a damp cold that worked its way through clothing slowly, patient and persistent.

Jonah barely noticed. He had spent enough time near the ocean to understand that winter along the Oregon coast had its own rhythm. Nothing moved quickly here in January. Boats creaked softly against their fenders. The tide shifted. Gulls drifted overhead in lazy circles, waiting.

The harbor master's office behind him buzzed with the faint sound of a radio playing somewhere inside. Jonah watched the water. It was something he had been doing more often lately. Since everything had happened.

The town of Seabrook looked mostly the same from the outside. The same narrow streets ran between weathered storefronts. The same fishing boats still came in before sunrise. The same gulls still gathered along the docks. But once you knew the truth about a place, it never quite looked the same again.

Jonah understood that now. A year ago he would have looked at Seabrook and seen a small coastal town where everyone knew each other's names. A place where things felt predictable. Safe. Now he saw something else beneath that surface. Secrets didn't disappear when they were uncovered. They simply left spaces behind.

Jonah shifted his weight slightly and glanced toward the harbor entrance where the ocean stretched out beyond the breakwater. The water out there was darker today, the surface broken into uneven patches by a steady wind pushing in from the west.

Behind him, a truck door slammed somewhere in the marina parking lot. Jonah didn't turn around. He had gotten used to listening without looking. Footsteps moved along the wooden dock behind him. Heavy boots. Slow pace. Someone carrying weight. The boards creaked in a familiar pattern that traveled ahead of the person walking. A moment later a voice called out.

"You planning to stand there all afternoon?"

Jonah glanced back. Detective Hale stood near the beginning of the dock with one hand resting on the railing. He wore the same dark jacket he always seemed to wear during the colder months, the collar turned slightly against the wind. His truck was parked near the marina office. Jonah shrugged slightly.

"Maybe."

Hale studied him for a moment, then walked a few steps farther along the dock. The boards creaked under his boots.

"You find anything interesting?" he asked.

Jonah looked back at the water.

"Not really."

Hale leaned against the railing beside him. For a moment neither of them spoke. The harbor moved quietly around them. A small workboat passed slowly along the far side of the marina, its engine humming steadily as it moved between rows of fishing vessels. The operator lifted a hand briefly toward Hale as he passed. Hale nodded in return.

"You skipped school again today," he said after a moment.

Jonah shifted slightly.

"I didn't skip."

Hale raised an eyebrow.

"You were absent."

"That's different."

"Is it?"

Jonah considered that for a second.

"Technically."

Hale watched him carefully for a moment longer but didn't push the issue. Living with Jonah over the past few months had taught him something important. If Jonah didn't want to answer a question, pushing usually didn't help.

"You're spending a lot of time down here lately," Hale said instead.

Jonah nodded slightly.

"I like the harbor."

"That so?"

Jonah shrugged.

"It's quiet."

Hale followed his gaze across the water. Winter had emptied the marina of most visitors. Only working boats remained now. Fishermen. Repair crews. Harbor maintenance. People who were used to the cold.

"Quiet can be good," Hale said.

Jonah didn't answer. He watched a gull drift slowly past overhead. Living at Hale's bluff house had taken some getting used to.

The house sat above the ocean just north of town, perched along a stretch of rocky coastline where waves crashed against dark cliffs below. From the back porch you could see the Pacific stretching endlessly toward the horizon.

It should have felt peaceful. Sometimes it did. Other times the quiet left too much room for thoughts Jonah wasn't sure what to do with yet. The wind shifted slightly, carrying a stronger smell of salt across the marina. Behind them, voices rose suddenly near the far end of the dock. Loud. Sharp.

Jonah turned his head slightly. Two men stood near one of the larger fishing boats tied along Dock C. One of them Jonah recognized immediately. Josh Hoggins.

Josh worked around the harbor doing whatever jobs people needed done. Loading gear. Cleaning decks. Moving equipment. The kind of work that never stayed the same from one day to the next. He had a reputation in Seabrook. Loud. Unreliable. Quick to argue. Jonah had seen him around the marina plenty of times. Josh's voice carried easily across the dock.

"I'm telling you that's not how it happened!"

The other man stood with his back partially turned toward Jonah. Derek Townsend. Owner of Townsend Marine Repair. Most of the boats in Seabrook eventually passed through Derek's shop at some point. Engine work. Electrical systems. Hull repairs.

Derek had built a good reputation over the years. Reliable. Professional. Jonah had heard people describe him that way more than once. Right now Derek stood calmly with his hands resting at his sides. His voice was much quieter than Josh's. Jonah couldn't hear the exact words. But the tone was steady. Controlled. Josh took a step closer.

"You think you can just tell people whatever story you want?"

Derek didn't move. Something in the air between them shifted. Jonah felt it immediately. Not just anger. Anger was loud. This was something else. Humiliation. The kind that sat deep beneath the surface. Josh's voice grew sharper.

"You don't get to decide how this goes."

Several fishermen nearby had started glancing over. Arguments weren't unusual around the marina. But something about this one held people's attention. Derek spoke again. Quiet. Calm. Whatever he said made Josh's face flush suddenly. Josh stepped forward like he might swing. For a moment it looked like he might. Then something stopped him. Josh exhaled sharply and shook his head.

"This isn't over," he muttered.

Derek didn't react. Josh turned abruptly and stormed down the dock toward the marina parking lot. His boots struck the wooden boards hard with each step. The sound faded quickly.

Silence returned to the harbor. Derek remained where he stood for another moment. Then he turned and walked calmly toward the ramp leading back to shore. Jonah watched him go. Something about the moment settled uneasily in his chest. Not the argument itself. Arguments happened everywhere. But the feeling beneath it. Jonah glanced toward Hale as he approached. The detective had also been watching Josh run toward the dock.

"What was that about?" Hale asked.

Jonah shook his head slowly.

"I'm not sure."

Hale studied Derek's retreating figure for a moment.

"Dock arguments happen all the time," he said.

Jonah nodded.

"I know."

But he kept watching Derek until the man disappeared up the ramp toward the marina lot. Something about the exchange lingered. The same way certain moments sometimes did. Small details. Pieces that didn't quite fit yet. Jonah turned back toward the water. The tide had begun to shift.

Far out past the breakwater, the Pacific rolled steadily toward shore beneath the low winter sky. Behind them, the harbor returned to its quiet rhythm. But somewhere in the back of Jonah's mind, a small thread had already begun to tighten. He just didn't know it yet.

Chapter 2

By the time the harbor lights flickered on, the sky had darkened to the color of old steel. Winter evenings settled early over Seabrook. By five o'clock the marina had already begun folding in on itself, the working day shrinking beneath a low ceiling of cloud and a cold wind that smelled like salt and wet rope. Yellow dock lamps threw thin reflections across the black water between slips. Somewhere farther out, a bell buoy clanged softly beyond the breakwater.

Jonah stood just inside the open door of the harbor master's office, warming his hands around a paper cup of coffee Hale had insisted on buying for him even though Jonah had told him twice he didn't really want it.

"You keep saying that," Hale had said. "Then you drink half of it anyway."

Now Jonah was doing exactly that.

The office was small and crowded in the way old marina buildings always seemed to be. A bulletin board on one wall held tide charts, weather advisories, and handwritten notices about engine parts, crab gear, and a missing tackle box no one had apparently claimed in three weeks. A small radio sat on the counter near the back window, murmuring static between bursts of country music. The room smelled like damp paper, diesel, and coffee strong enough to take paint off wood.

Hale stood near the counter speaking with Pete Landry, the harbor master. Pete was a thick-shouldered man in his sixties with a gray beard and the weathered skin of someone who had spent more of his life outside than in. He wore a knit cap pulled low over his forehead and a heavy flannel shirt under a faded rain jacket. He had the same expression most harbor men seemed born with, part suspicion, part exhaustion.

"I'm not saying anything happened," Pete was saying. "I'm

saying Josh has disappeared before."

Hale leaned one shoulder against the counter. "For this long?"

Pete shrugged. "Depends what you call long."

"How about more than a day?"

Pete glanced toward the window overlooking the slips. "Sometimes."

Jonah took another small sip of coffee and watched the marina through the glass. A gull landed on the roof of a bait shack and stood there hunched against the wind, looking faintly annoyed at the entire season.

The argument from earlier still sat in the back of Jonah's mind. Josh Hoggins, red-faced and loud. Derek Townsend, still as a fence post. The thing Jonah hadn't stopped thinking about wasn't the shouting itself. It was the way Derek had stood there afterward. Not rattled. Not angry. Just composed. Like whatever had happened had landed exactly where he expected it to. Pete rubbed a hand across his beard.

"Josh gets mad," he said. "Josh drinks. Josh mouths off. Sometimes he sleeps on somebody's boat and shows up the next day pretending nothing happened. Nobody calls the police every time Josh Hoggins misses breakfast."

Hale's expression didn't change. "Did he have work today?"

"Deck cleanup on the Merriweather. Then a delivery run of bait crates around noon." Pete paused. "Didn't show."

"Who noticed first?"

"Eli."

Hale glanced toward the open office door. "He still around?"

Pete nodded. "Out by the fuel dock."

Hale pushed off the counter. "I'll talk to him."

Pete grunted and took a sip from his own mug. "Tell him not to dramatize it. That boy could make a dropped wrench sound like a shipwreck."

Hale gave Jonah a brief look on his way past the door. "You coming?"

Jonah nodded and followed him back out into the cold.

The marina had thinned out since earlier, but it wasn't empty.

A few men still worked the slips in jackets and knit caps, coiling lines, checking lights, moving gear into covered bins before the temperature dropped further overnight. The harbor beyond them had gone almost black now, only the chop of the water catching bits of reflected light.

They found Eli near the fuel dock loading plastic bins into the bed of a pickup. He looked about twenty-two, maybe twenty-three, with dark hair shoved under a Seahawks beanie and the nervous energy of someone who talked even when no one had asked him anything yet. He turned when he heard footsteps.

"Oh. Hey, Detective."

Hale stopped a few feet away. "You're Eli?"

"Yeah."

"You were looking for Josh today?"

Eli nodded quickly. "Yeah, because he was supposed to help me unload gear off the Darlene Mae this morning, and when he didn't show I figured maybe he overslept somewhere, but then his truck was still here."

He pointed across the lot. Jonah followed the motion and saw it immediately. An older blue pickup sat alone near the far edge of the parking area, backed crookedly into a space beside a stack of crab pots. Rain streaks marked the doors. One rear tire looked slightly low.

"Been there since last night?" Hale asked.

Eli nodded again. "Pretty sure."

"You sure?"

"I mean, as sure as I can be. I was here before sunrise. Truck was here then."

Hale looked toward the pickup. "Keys inside?"

"Don't know. I didn't check."

"You know if Josh took a boat out?"

Eli let out a breath through his nose and gave the kind of half-shrug that meant yes, no, and maybe all at once.

"That's what everybody's saying."

"Everybody meaning who?"

Eli shifted a bin in the truck bed. "Just... people."

Hale waited. Eli glanced past him toward the slips and lowered his voice a little.

"Look, Josh drinks, okay? Everybody knows that. Sometimes he gets this idea in his head that he can still run a skiff better after six beers than most people can sober."

Hale said nothing.

Eli added, "Not smart. Just true."

Jonah watched his face while he said it. There wasn't much fear there. Mostly irritation. The kind people carried when they were already tired of defending a missing person's worst habits.

"You think he took a boat out drunk and fell off," Hale said.

Eli hesitated, then nodded once. "Wouldn't be the first dumb thing he's done."

The words hung in the air a second too long. Jonah looked toward the slips. A gull cried somewhere in the dark. Rope tapped rhythmically against a mast. Beyond the fuel dock, several small skiffs rocked in place, tied neatly where they belonged. No obvious empty slip. No clear sign that someone had taken a boat without permission. Hale seemed to notice the same thing.

"What boat?"

Eli blinked. "What?"

"If he went out," Hale said, "what boat did he take?"

Eli opened his mouth, then closed it again.

"I mean... maybe one of the small skiffs."

"Whose?"

Another pause. Jonah felt it then. Not exactly a lie. More like assumption hardening into certainty because it sounded plausible.

Eli scratched the back of his neck. "I don't know. Somebody probably knows."

Hale gave a short nod, not unfriendly.

"Who saw Josh last?"

Eli looked toward the parking lot again.

"Not me."

"Who, then?"

Eli hesitated. "I heard he got into it with somebody yesterday."

Jonah's attention sharpened slightly.

"With who?" Hale asked.

Eli looked like he was debating whether he wanted to be part of this conversation anymore.

"Don't know for sure," he said. "Just heard there was shouting down near Dock C."

Hale glanced at Jonah.

Jonah said, "I saw the argument."

Eli looked at him, surprised. "You did?"

Jonah nodded once.

"Who was it with?" Hale asked.

Jonah held his gaze. "Derek Townsend."

The name seemed to land oddly in the cold air.

Eli frowned. "Derek?"

"Yeah."

"Townsend Marine Derek?"

Jonah almost smiled at the phrasing. In a town the size of Seabrook, people often identified each other by function as much as name.

"The same one," Hale said.

Eli looked genuinely surprised now. "Huh."

"What?" Hale asked.

"I just... I don't know." Eli shrugged again. "Derek doesn't really yell."

Jonah thought neither had Josh, not really. Not at first. That was part of what had felt off. Derek had stayed so calm that Josh had been forced to carry the entire emotional weight of the argument by himself.

"What were they arguing about?" Hale asked Jonah.

"I couldn't hear everything."

"What could you hear?"

Jonah looked back toward Dock C. The boards there were dark with damp, the railings shining faintly under the lamps.

"Josh said, 'That's not how it happened.' And something about Derek telling people whatever story he wanted."

Hale's eyes narrowed slightly, not with suspicion but focus.

"That all?"

Jonah nodded. "Mostly."

Eli shifted his weight. "That's weird."

Hale turned. "Why weird?"

Eli seemed to regret saying it as soon as the detective looked at him.

"Just... Derek and Josh don't really run in the same circles."

Hale let that sit for a second.

"Meaning?"

"Meaning Josh is Josh. Derek's..." Eli waved a hand vaguely toward the repair sheds. "Different."

Calm. Respected. Professional. Jonah had heard all those words before.

Hale asked a few more questions, none of which got them much farther. No one had seen Josh leave the marina. No one could say for certain he took a boat. No one had checked his truck. The entire situation still floated in that strange space between concern and inconvenience.

Finally Hale said, "Show me the truck."

They crossed the lot with Eli trailing a few steps behind. Up close, the pickup looked even more forgotten. A coffee cup sat in the dashboard tray. A torn rain jacket was balled up on the passenger seat. One of the wipers was lifted slightly off the glass like it had been caught that way by the wind.

Eli peered through the driver's side window. "Yep. Same old disaster."

Hale tried the door handle. Locked. He circled slowly around the truck, light from the lot lamps striping across the wet metal.

"No obvious damage," he said.

Jonah stood near the tailgate and looked at the bed. A yellow bucket. Coiled rope. One muddy boot lying on its side near a crate of rusted tools. Only one boot. His eyes stayed on it for a second. Hale noticed.

"What?"

Jonah nodded toward the truck bed. "Just one."

Hale followed his gaze. "Maybe the other's in the cab."

"Maybe."

But the single boot bothered him anyway. Not because it proved anything. Just because missing things often bothered him before he knew why. Hale spoke with Pete again. Then with two more dock workers and an older shrimper named Lowell who insisted three separate times that Josh had no sense and even less luck. All of them repeated some version of the same general theory.

If Josh was gone, he was probably gone because Josh had done something dumb. Taken a skiff out. Passed out somewhere. Fallen off a dock. Started a fight. Slept it off. It was remarkable how quickly people could turn a missing man into a pattern they already understood.

By the time darkness had settled fully over the marina, the radio chatter in the harbor office had shifted from weather and boat traffic to low, casual speculation. Someone mentioned the Coast Guard. Someone else said that was overkill unless there was actual evidence Josh went out on the water. Someone else said evidence wasn't exactly Josh's style.

Jonah stayed quiet. He stood once more near the edge of Dock C, looking at the black water slapping gently against pilings below. Hale joined him a minute later.

"You thinking?" Hale asked.

Jonah nodded.

"That obvious?"

"Yes."

Jonah kept his eyes on the water.

"Everyone already decided what happened."

"People like easy explanations," Hale said.

"That doesn't mean they're wrong."

Jonah thought about that. It was true. Sometimes the simplest explanation really was the right one. A drunk man with a bad reputation disappears near boats and cold water. You didn't have to be imaginative to draw a line. Still.

"What?" Hale asked.

Jonah glanced toward the lot where Josh's truck still sat alone under the lights.

"I don't know," he said. "Something about it feels too settled."

Hale looked at him. "Settled how?"

"Like people were ready for him to disappear before he actually did."

The detective was quiet a moment. Wind moved across the harbor, lifting the smell of tidewater and diesel between them. Somewhere farther down the marina, a halyard tapped metal in an uneven rhythm. Hale rested his forearms on the railing and looked out toward the breakwater.

"You know what the problem is with men like Josh?" he said.

Jonah waited.

"Eventually everybody starts seeing the worst thing they've done as the only thing they're capable of doing."

Jonah looked down at the dark water below.

"And then when something happens to them..."

"They don't get the benefit of uncertainty," Hale finished.

For a moment neither of them spoke. Then Hale straightened.

"I'm not opening an official missing persons case tonight."

Jonah nodded. That made sense. No body. No witness. No boat. Just absence.

"But," Hale added, "I am going to keep asking questions."

Jonah looked at him.

"About Derek?"

Hale's expression stayed neutral. "About everybody."

Which meant yes, at least a little. A truck engine started somewhere near the fuel dock. Men were heading home now. Harbor noise was changing shape, becoming smaller, more hollow. The workday had ended. The marina was slipping into nighttime. Jonah shoved his hands deeper into his jacket pockets.

"You think he took a boat?" Hale asked.

Jonah considered the question carefully.

"I think everybody wants him to have."

Hale looked at him for a second, then nodded once as if that was a fair answer. They started walking back toward the lot. Halfway there, Jonah slowed.

"What now?"

He pointed toward the far end of the slips, beyond the repair sheds where the dock lights got thinner and the shadows deeper. Hale followed his gaze. At first Jonah thought it was just movement in the dark. Then he saw it again.

A figure near one of the outer slips. Someone standing beside a boat with a flashlight held low, the beam briefly cutting across wet boards before vanishing again. The person moved quickly, untied something, then bent out of sight. Hale stopped.

"Stay here."

He started down the dock at once, boots striking the boards hard enough now that stealth clearly wasn't the goal. Jonah remained where he was, though every part of him wanted to follow. The flashlight vanished.

A second later came the sound of an engine turning over. Small, but immediate. Hale broke into a run. The boat emerged from the darkness at the far edge of the slips, just a low skiff with a single stern light flickering weakly as it swung out into the channel. Whoever was inside didn't look back.

The detective stopped at the end of the dock, too far now. The skiff was already moving out past the outer line of boats, heading toward the harbor mouth. By the time Jonah reached him, the boat had become little more than a shape gliding through black water beneath the winter sky.

"Who was it?" Jonah asked.

Hale kept watching the channel.

"I don't know."

"You think it was Josh?"

Hale didn't answer immediately. The skiff continued toward open water.

"No," he said at last.

Jonah looked at him. "Why not?"

Hale's eyes stayed fixed on the disappearing light.

"Because whoever that was," he said quietly, "they didn't want to be seen."

The boat slid farther into the dark until even its stern light disappeared beyond the breakwater. The harbor fell quiet again. But the night didn't feel settled anymore. And somewhere in that darkness beyond Seabrook's marina, a boat had just gone out when everyone was supposed to believe Josh Hoggins had already been gone all along.

Chapter 3

The next morning Seabrook looked as though the sun had forgotten it existed. A pale gray sky hung over the town, low and heavy, blurring the tops of the pines beyond the school and flattening the color out of everything below. The sidewalks still held damp patches from overnight mist, and the air had that familiar winter sharpness that smelled faintly of salt and cedar bark.

Jonah stood near the front entrance of Ember Lane High with both hands in the pockets of his jacket, watching students move past him in uneven currents. Most of them looked half-awake.

A few laughed too loudly about something that probably hadn't been funny even before first period. Someone dropped a binder near the front steps. Somewhere behind him, a car stereo pulsed briefly before a door slammed shut and the sound disappeared. The day looked normal. That was part of what bothered him.

He had spent enough time around investigations now to know that strange things almost never announced themselves properly. They happened quietly. Then the world continued around them anyway. School bells still rang. The coffee shop still opened. Boats still moved in and out of the harbor.

Meanwhile, somewhere beyond all of that, a man might be missing. Or drunk. Or dead. Jonah shifted his weight slightly and looked toward the parking lot. He hadn't told anyone at school what he and Hale had seen the night before. The skiff leaving the marina. The flashlight. The way the boat had moved out into the dark as if it had someplace very specific to go.

Even thinking about it now made something uneasy move in his chest. Not fear exactly. More like incompletion. A thread left hanging.

"Let me guess," a voice said beside him. "You've been standing here five minutes pretending not to think about whatever you're obviously thinking about."

Jonah glanced over. Mara Ellison stood with her backpack slung over one shoulder and a coffee cup in one hand. Her hair was pulled into a loose braid that had already started slipping apart in the damp air. A few strands had curled free near her face. She looked more awake than most people did this early, though that might have had more to do with stubbornness than sleep. Jonah looked back toward the school entrance.

"I'm waiting for the bell."

Mara took a sip from her coffee.

"Sure."

They stood in silence for a moment while a group of freshmen hurried up the steps arguing about a biology quiz. Jonah watched them disappear inside.

Then Mara said, "You were at the harbor last night."

It wasn't a question. Jonah glanced at her.

"How do you know that?"

Mara gave him a flat look.

"Because your version of 'I'm fine' gets quieter when you've been around Hale too long."

Jonah almost smiled.

"That's not a real thing."

"It absolutely is."

The first warning bell rang overhead, buzzing across the front of the school. Students began moving faster now, conversations shortening as people turned toward classrooms and lockers. Mara lowered her cup.

"So?"

Jonah looked ahead for another second before answering.

"Hale was asking around about Josh Hoggins."

"The dock guy?"

"Yeah."

"What happened?"

Jonah hesitated. Then: "He didn't show up for work."

Mara's expression shifted slightly.

"That bad?"

"Maybe."

They started walking inside with the rest of the students. The warm, stale air of the building met them immediately, carrying the mixed scent of wet jackets, floor cleaner, and cafeteria toast that somehow always made the front hallway smell faintly wrong in the mornings.

Lockers banged open and shut. Someone down the corridor laughed so hard they snorted. A teacher near the English wing reminded a student for the third time to remove his hood.

Everything at school operated by repetition. Same bells. Same announcements. Same fluorescent hum overhead. Jonah usually liked that about it. Today it only made him feel more separated from everyone else moving through it. Mara noticed.

"You think something happened to him."

Jonah opened his locker.

"I don't know."

"That wasn't my statement."

Jonah pulled out a notebook and shut the locker door. Mara waited. He glanced around the hallway before lowering his voice slightly.

"Somebody took a boat out of the marina late last night."

Her eyebrows rose.

"What?"

"I saw it with Hale."

"Who?"

Jonah shook his head.

"We couldn't tell."

Mara looked at him carefully now.

"And you're just opening with that?"

"You asked."

"I did not ask in a way that implied secret nighttime boat departures."

Jonah shrugged slightly. "Fair."

They started walking toward first period. Mara kept her voice low.

"You think it was Josh?"

"No."

She looked at him sideways.

"How do you know?"

Jonah thought about Hale standing at the end of the dock, watching the skiff disappear past the breakwater. Because whoever that was, they didn't want to be seen.

"I don't," Jonah said. "Not really. But it didn't feel like someone drunk."

Mara frowned.

"What does that mean?"

"It means," Jonah said, searching for the right words, "if somebody takes a boat out drunk, that kind of mistake usually looks messy before it leaves."

"Messy?"

"Noise. Hesitation. Wrong rope. Wrong timing. Something."

Mara studied him for a second longer.

"And this didn't?"

"No."

They turned the corner near the science wing. Through the windows along the far wall, Jonah could see the Oregon sky hanging flat and colorless above the treeline. Beyond that sat the harbor, then the breakwater, then the Pacific pushing in beneath the clouds. A place could feel very far away even when it was only a few minutes from school.

"What does Hale think?" Mara asked.

Jonah hesitated.

"He thinks people are settling on a story too fast."

"That Josh got drunk and fell off a boat."

"Yeah."

Mara made a face.

"Charming."

"It's the easy version."

"And easy versions are usually wrong."

Jonah glanced at her.

"You sound confident."

Mara adjusted the strap of her backpack.

"I've known you for ten years. If you're this weird about it already, the easy version is definitely wrong."

He didn't answer that. The hallway had begun thinning as students slipped into classrooms. Their footsteps echoed a little more now. Somewhere upstairs, another bell buzzed softly in one wing before cutting off. Mara slowed near her classroom door.

"You telling anyone else?"

"No."

"Good."

Jonah raised an eyebrow.

"That seems like an odd response."

Mara lowered her voice.

"If there's actually something wrong, then the last thing Seabrook needs is twenty-seven versions of it by lunch."

That was fair. In towns like Seabrook, rumor spread the way fog moved through streets near the harbor. Quietly at first. Then everywhere all at once. Jonah nodded once.

"See you later."

Mara pushed open the classroom door.

"Try not to become unofficially involved in a criminal investigation before third period."

Jonah looked at her.

"I make no promises."

She gave him a small smile and disappeared inside.

By lunch the weather had worsened. Not rain exactly. More like a fine gray mist that had begun collecting on windows and darkening the blacktop outside. Students pressed through the cafeteria line carrying trays and complaints in roughly equal measure. The whole room buzzed with overlapping noise, louder than it deserved to be.

Jonah sat with Mara near the far side of the cafeteria, where the windows looked out toward the athletic fields now fading into the mist. His tray sat mostly untouched in front of him. Mara had noticed.

"Okay," she said. "That's officially concerning."

Jonah looked up.

"What is?"
"You're ignoring fries."
He glanced down.
"I'm eating."
"You moved one."
"That still counts."
Mara leaned back in her chair.
"So what else did Hale find?"
Jonah shook his head.
"Not much."
"Truck still there?"
"Yeah."
"Any sign Josh actually took a boat?"
"No."
She frowned slightly.
"So people just decided he did."
Jonah nodded.
"That's basically it."

At the next table over, two juniors were arguing about whether the basketball team could still make district if they beat Astoria on Friday. Behind them, someone dropped a fork. Near the vending machines, a cluster of sophomores stood in a circle around a phone watching something that made one of them say "No way" three times in a row. Normal noise.

Jonah found himself listening for pieces of the other thing. The harbor. Josh. The skiff. He heard it a few seconds later. Not from the students around him. From two teachers standing near the cafeteria doors with paper cups in their hands.

"...probably sleeping it off somewhere," one said quietly.

The other gave a small shrug.

"If he took one of those skiffs out last night, he's lucky if he only ends up wet."

Jonah looked at Mara. She had heard it too.

"So now teachers know," she said.

"Yeah."

"Which means by seventh period everyone will."

Jonah glanced toward the windows again. Mist beaded against the glass, blurring the field beyond into a pale gray wash.

"What if he didn't take a boat at all?" Mara asked.

Jonah turned back.

"That's what bothers me."

She lowered her voice.

"The boat you saw last night..."

Jonah nodded slightly.

"What if that wasn't Josh leaving," she said. "What if it was someone after?"

He didn't answer right away. Because that thought had already occurred to him somewhere around first period, and he hadn't liked it any better the second time. Mara watched his face.

"You already thought of that."

Jonah looked down at his tray.

"Yeah."

She was quiet a moment.

Then: "Did Hale?"

"I think so."

That didn't seem to comfort either of them much. The lunch bell rang a few minutes later. Chairs scraped back. Conversations broke apart. The cafeteria dissolved into motion again as students slung backpacks over shoulders and drifted back into the hallways.

Jonah and Mara moved with the crowd. At the far end of the corridor, a television mounted high in the corner near the library entrance played local midday news with the sound muted. The screen showed footage of the Seabrook harbor under gray skies. Jonah stopped walking. Mara followed his gaze. The banner at the bottom of the screen read:

HARBOR WORKER MISSING, SEARCH NOT YET OFFICIAL

A reporter stood outside the marina with wind pushing at her hair while a cameraman panned briefly across slips and fuel docks behind her.

"Wow," Mara said quietly. "That escalated."

Jonah stared at the screen. No audio. Just image. But that was enough. Once local news got hold of a story, it stopped belonging only to the people inside it. Students had begun noticing now too. A few slowed. One boy near the library looked up at the TV, then pulled out his phone immediately.

"It's out," Mara said.

Jonah nodded.

"Yeah."

The hallway felt subtly different now. Still school. Still lockers and announcements and shoes squeaking on tile. But beneath it all sat a fresh note of tension. Curiosity mixing with unease. Mara spoke quietly.

"Does Hale know they ran it already?"

"He probably told them enough to keep them calm."

"You have a very generous opinion of local news."

Jonah almost smiled at that. Almost. They kept walking. By the time final bell rang, the mist had thickened into a steady fine rain.

Students poured out of the building in clusters, ducking heads beneath jackets and backpacks as they crossed the parking lot toward buses and cars. Tires hissed over wet pavement beyond the curb. Somewhere behind the gym, a whistle blew twice and was swallowed immediately by weather. Jonah pulled up his hood and started down the front steps. Mara caught up beside him.

"You going home?"

Jonah hesitated.

Then: "Probably not first."

She nodded as if that was exactly what she expected.

"The harbor?"

"Yeah."

Mara tucked her hands deeper into the pockets of her coat.

"Tell Hale I said he's doing a bad job of keeping you out of things."

Jonah glanced at her.

"He knows."

"Good."

They reached the sidewalk where their paths split. Mara stopped and looked back toward the school for a second, then toward the washed-out sky beyond town.

"This feels bad," she said.

Not dramatic. Not exaggerated. Just honest. Jonah followed her gaze toward the unseen harbor.

"Yeah."

Mara looked at him.

"Be careful."

He nodded once. Then she turned and headed toward the student lot, braid darkening in the rain as she went. Jonah watched her for a moment before starting down Harbor Road.

The town looked quieter in this kind of weather. Storefront windows glowed warmer against the gray. The coffee shop on the corner had fogged glass and three people sitting inside with cups between their hands. Farther down the block, the bait shop's OPEN sign buzzed faintly in the window.

He passed the diner and caught sight of the harbor between buildings. Even from here he could feel the shift in the place. News crews. Speculation. Concern trying to pretend it was still casual.

By the time Jonah reached the marina, the rain had eased back to mist. Hale's truck was parked beside the harbor office again. Jonah found him under the awning near the fuel dock, speaking with Pete Landry while both men stared out at the slips. Hale looked over as Jonah approached.

"You done with school?"

"For today."

Hale gave him a look. "That phrasing is suspicious."

Jonah stopped beside them. Pete grunted.

"You kids hear about things faster than radios now."

Jonah glanced toward the outer slips.

"Any sign of him?"

Hale shook his head once.

"No."

The detective looked tired in a way that had nothing to do

with sleep. More like the shape of the day had already settled on his shoulders and wasn't likely to lighten by nightfall.

"Still informal?" Jonah asked.

"For the moment."

Pete folded his arms against the cold.

"Coast Guard called back," he said. "They'll do a look around the harbor mouth if we make enough noise about it, but they're not treating it like a recovery unless we get something firmer."

Jonah watched the water. Black, shifting, restless beneath the dimming afternoon.

"What about the boat from last night?" he asked.

Hale was quiet a beat too long.

"Still working on it."

That meant no answer yet. Or not one he wanted to share. Pete pushed open the harbor office door behind him and disappeared inside, leaving Jonah and Hale alone beneath the awning. Rain tapped softly against the metal roof overhead.

"News got it," Jonah said.

"I know."

"You don't seem surprised."

Hale looked out across the slips.

"In small towns, once three people know something, it's already halfway to camera-ready."

Jonah leaned lightly against a damp railing post.

"Do you think he's dead?"

Hale didn't answer immediately. The harbor beyond them rocked and clicked in the fading light. Somewhere a loose line knocked rhythmically against fiberglass. A gull stood in the rain on top of a piling like a disapproving landlord.

Finally Hale said, "I think people can go missing for a lot of reasons."

That was not an answer. Jonah looked at him.

Hale met his eyes, saw the thought, and added quietly, "And I think guessing too early helps no one."

That was closer. Jonah nodded once. Not because he was satisfied. Because he understood. The detective shifted his attention back toward the marina.

"You notice anything at school?"

Jonah hesitated.

"Like what?"

"People talk."

"So do dock workers."

Hale almost smiled.

"Fair."

Jonah thought about the teachers near the cafeteria doors. The television near the library. The way rumor had already taken on shape before the facts had.

"Mostly people think he got drunk and fell off a boat."

Hale's expression went still again.

"Yeah."

Jonah looked out toward the harbor mouth where the skiff had disappeared the night before.

"I still don't think that's what happened."

Rain moved across the water in faint silver streaks. Hale followed his gaze.

"Neither do I."

It was the first time he'd said it plainly. Jonah felt the words settle into place. Not a solution. Not even a clue, really. Just confirmation that the easy explanation had started cracking. The two of them stood there in silence for another minute, listening to the harbor breathe around them.

Then, out near the far slips, a boat horn sounded once. Short. Hollow. Lonely in the mist. And for reasons Jonah couldn't explain yet, the sound made the marina feel much larger than it had that morning. Larger. And emptier. And full of things no one was saying.

Chapter 4

The rain tapered off just before dusk, leaving the marina slick and reflective under the harbor lights. Water clung to the rails, pooled in the grooves between dock planks, and dripped steadily from the edges of awnings and cabin roofs. The air had grown colder with the clearing sky, and out beyond the breakwater the ocean had darkened into a single flat line beneath the last smear of gray light.

Jonah stood beside Hale near the fuel dock and watched a forklift back slowly away from a stack of bait crates. Its warning beep echoed thinly across the harbor before cutting off. A gull landed on the roof of the harbor office, shook rain from its wings, and settled in like it owned the place. Pete Landry stepped back out beneath the awning with a clipboard in one hand and a mug in the other.

"Harbor cams are useless," he muttered. "Outer slip camera's been cutting in and out for two weeks. Rear lot one sees about half the driveway and a seagull with bad intentions."

Hale took the clipboard from him and scanned it.

"You got boat assignments for last night?"

"Mostly." Pete sipped from his mug. "Anything official yet?"

"Not yet."

Pete grunted as though that answer satisfied and annoyed him at the same time. Jonah looked across the marina toward the repair sheds. Most of the small businesses along the harbor had already gone dark for the night, but one building still held light behind the windows.

Townsend Marine Repair.

The sign above the bay doors looked pale under the lamps, the letters catching the moisture in the air. The front office light glowed warm and steady. Hale followed Jonah's gaze.

"Come on," he said.

Pete looked up. "You heading over there?"

"Yeah."

Pete scratched at his beard.

"For what it's worth, Townsend's usually still here late."

"Good," Hale said.

They crossed the lot in silence. The puddles reflected yellow and white in broken shapes beneath their feet. Somewhere behind them, a halyard tapped metal in a slow irregular rhythm. Beyond the slips, the harbor mouth sat dark and quiet, the same channel where the skiff had disappeared the night before. Jonah kept thinking about that light vanishing into open water. Not because it was dramatic. Because it had felt deliberate.

Townsend Marine Repair occupied a long rectangular building near the far edge of the marina lot. Two service bays sat open but empty, the concrete floor inside was wet in places from boots and tracked-in rain. Racks of tools hung in clean lines along the back wall. Spare engine parts sat labeled on shelves. A half-disassembled outboard motor rested on a stand near one of the bays under a hanging work lamp.

The whole place looked orderly in a way that stood out sharply against the rest of the marina. Even the grease seemed organized. The office door stood open. Derek Townsend looked up from behind the front counter as Hale and Jonah stepped in. For a brief second his expression held only surprise. Then it settled into something calm and professional.

"Detective," he said. "Evening."

He glanced at Jonah and nodded once.

"Jonah."

Derek had changed since the argument. Or maybe not changed. Reset. He wore a dark sweater under a work jacket; the sleeves pushed neatly to his forearms. His hair was dry now, combed back from his face. He looked like a man finishing paperwork after a long but manageable day. Nothing about him suggested someone fraying at the edges. Hale stopped at the counter.

"Still open?"

Derek gave a faint smile.

"Depends how much work you're bringing me."

"Just questions."

The smile didn't leave. "Those are usually cheaper."

Jonah watched him carefully.

If Derek felt any real tension at seeing them, it didn't show in the obvious ways. His breathing stayed even. Shoulders relaxed. Voice steady. Calm. Professional. Exactly what people said he was. Hale rested one hand lightly against the counter.

"You heard Josh Hoggins hasn't shown up."

Derek nodded.

"I heard."

"From who?"

"Pete, about an hour ago." He hesitated just enough to be natural. "I figured somebody would start asking around."

Hale said, "You knew him well?"

Derek gave a small shrug.

"Well enough. Harbor guy. Everybody knows everybody at least a little."

That was true. In Seabrook, people accumulated around each other the way salt accumulated on old pilings. Quietly. Over time. Derek folded a service invoice in half and set it aside.

"I assume this is partly about yesterday," he said.

Hale looked at him. "Yesterday?"

"The argument."

He said it without resistance, without waiting to be cornered into it. Just offered it up like someone trying to save everyone time. Jonah felt something ease in his own thinking without meaning to. Guilty people usually hid obvious things first. Derek had just stepped directly toward one.

"You and Josh argued on Dock C," Hale said.

Derek nodded once. "We did."

"About?"

Derek let out a quiet breath through his nose and leaned one hip against the counter.

"Josh thought I'd told someone at the harbor he'd damaged a

winch line on one of the charter rigs last month."

"Had you?" Hale asked.

A tiny smile crossed Derek's face, tired more than amused. "Yes."

The answer came easily.

"Because he had damaged it," Derek continued. "And the owner asked me why the replacement job took longer than expected. I told him the truth."

Hale waited.

"Josh didn't like that."

"No."

Jonah thought back to the argument. That's not how it happened.

You think you can just tell people whatever story you want?

Derek's explanation fit those words neatly enough that Jonah felt mildly annoyed at how reasonable it sounded.

Hale asked, "Did things get physical?"

"No."

"Threats?"

Derek thought for a second.

"Depends how broadly you define threats."

"Try me."

Derek folded his arms.

"He said it wasn't over."

"That all?"

"More or less."

He didn't embellish. Didn't dramatize. Didn't try too hard to minimize it either. It was, Jonah had to admit, a very believable version of events. Hale glanced toward the service bays, then back at Derek.

"When did you last see him?"

"After the argument. He stormed off toward the lot."

"Did he seem drunk?"

Derek shook his head. "No."

That answer registered somewhere in Jonah immediately. Everyone else in the harbor had started leaning on Josh's drinking like it was structural support. Derek didn't. Not because he was defending Josh. Because the question had been too specific to dodge lazily. Hale seemed to notice too.

"You hear the theory he took a boat out?"

Derek's expression changed only slightly. Not suspicion. More like distaste.

"I heard people saying it."

"You believe it?"

Derek paused.

"I believe Josh was capable of doing reckless things," he said carefully. "I don't know if he did this one."

Again, annoyingly reasonable. Jonah's eyes drifted past the counter toward a laminated chart pinned to the wall near the office door. Tide tables. Harbor service routes. A faded map of the nearshore waters with handwritten circles around maintenance zones and winter markers.

Off to one side, almost like an afterthought, several tiny islands were marked just beyond the main harbor routes. Seasonal notations sat beside them in faded pen. Crab sheds. Storage. Restricted access in storms. Jonah looked away before Derek noticed him studying it.

Hale said, "Anyone you know who Josh was meeting last night?"

Derek shook his head.

"No."

"Anyone he'd been having trouble with besides you?"

This time Derek seemed to consider the answer a little longer.

"Josh had trouble with a lot of people," he said. "That's not the same as enemies."

Hale didn't interrupt.

Derek added, "He'd been bouncing around jobs. Late on things. Borrowing money, depending on who you ask."

Jonah watched Hale absorb that without reaction.

Then Derek said, "You might want to talk to Calvin Rudd."

Jonah's attention sharpened.

Hale asked, "Why?"

Derek rested both hands on the counter now.

"Because Josh and Calvin got into it a few days ago."

"When?"

"Late morning, I think. Near the bait lockers."

"What about?"

Derek shook his head. "Couldn't hear the whole thing. But it looked worse than mine."

That landed heavily and neatly at once. A suspect. A cleaner one than Derek.

Hale's voice stayed neutral. "Physical?"

"I saw shoving."

"Who started it?"

Derek gave a small shrug.

"With those two? Hard to say."

He didn't push the point. Didn't over-sell it. He just placed the information there and let it sit. Jonah felt something subtle move beneath the surface of the conversation. Not a lie, exactly. More like usefulness. Derek was being helpful in the most efficient possible way. Hale glanced down at the paperwork scattered near the counter.

"You here late last night?"

"Until about eight."

"Anyone confirm that?"

Derek nodded toward the open service bay.

"Danny Mercer was with me until a little after seven-thirty. Then I finished paperwork and closed up."

"Go straight home?"

"Yes."

It came without hesitation. Hale asked a few more questions. Routine ones. About Josh's habits. About access to skiffs. About harbor keys and who tended to stay late during winter. Derek answered them all with the same measured steadiness. Nothing too polished. Nothing too defensive.

Just enough detail to sound like a man cooperating because he believed that was the sensible thing to do. When they finally stepped back outside, the temperature had dropped another few degrees. Their breath showed faintly now in the damp evening air.

The marina lot looked darker than before, the wet pavement swallowing more of the light. Jonah walked beside Hale without speaking at first.

Finally Hale said, "Well?"

Jonah looked ahead.

"He was honest about the argument."

"Yeah."

"That helps him."

"It does."

Jonah thought about Derek bringing it up himself before Hale had mentioned it. That mattered. It had felt open. Practical. Not the move of somebody trying to hide a confrontation.

"He also didn't jump on the drunk boat story," Jonah said.

Hale glanced at him.

"You noticed that."

"Yeah."

"So did I."

They kept walking toward the harbor office. Near the fuel dock, a pair of deckhands were unloading coolers from the back of a truck while arguing lazily about football. Someone laughed near the bait shed. For a place sitting under the possibility of a missing man, the marina still kept trying to be itself. Maybe that was what towns did best. Not noticing. Or noticing only as much that let them keep going.

Halfway back to the office, Jonah said, "Do you think Calvin actually fought him?"

Hale shoved his hands into his jacket pockets.

"Probably."

"You believe Derek?"

"About that part? Maybe."

Jonah frowned slightly.

"That's not very specific."

"It's also accurate."

They reached the awning outside the harbor office. Pete was gone now. A radio played softly inside. Someone had left a desk lamp on, casting a warm square of light across a stack of tide sheets. Hale stopped beside one of the outer windows.

"Here's the thing," he said. "People can tell the truth for all kinds of reasons."

Jonah waited.

"Sometimes because they're honest," Hale continued. "Sometimes because that piece of truth helps them more than hiding it would."

Jonah looked back toward Townsend Marine Repair. The office light still glowed inside.

"So being honest doesn't mean he's clear."

"No."

"But it also doesn't mean he's lying."

Hale nodded. "Exactly."

That was the annoying part of investigations, Jonah thought. Everyone wanted certainty to arrive dressed like certainty. Instead it usually showed up disguised as small contradictions and people being almost normal.

A truck pulled into the marina lot then, slower than the others, its headlights sweeping damp light across the office windows before cutting off. A broad man climbed out wearing an old canvas coat and a knit watch cap. Even from this distance Jonah could feel the shape of his mood before he saw his face clearly.

Irritation. Not guilt. Not fear. Just the heavy blunt annoyance of someone who didn't want to be here and expected the world to make that everyone else's problem too. The man slammed the truck door and started toward the office. Hale glanced over.

"Looks like rumor travels fast."

Jonah looked at him. "That's Calvin?"

"Has to be."

Calvin Rudd crossed the lot with a stiff, purposeful stride. He was older than Jonah had expected, maybe late thirties, with a thick beard and shoulders that made his coat seem too small through the chest. His boots left dark prints across the wet pavement. He stopped under the awning, looked at Hale, then at Jonah.

"You asking around about Josh?" he said.

No greeting. No setup.

Hale straightened slightly.

"Who's asking?"

Calvin let out a rough breath through his nose.

"Pete called my cousin. My cousin called me. Now I'm here, which I assume saves you a drive."

His voice carried the strained control of someone trying not to start a second fight simply because he was standing near one.

Hale said, "We heard you and Josh had words."

Calvin gave a short humorless laugh.

"Had more than words."

Jonah felt the emotional weight shift immediately. Frustration. Resentment. And underneath it, something harder to pin down. Not sorrow. Not concern. Something closer to old aggravation.

"When?" Hale asked.

"Couple of days ago. Before noon."

"About?"

Calvin looked past them toward the harbor, then back again.

"Money."

"Josh owed you?"

"He owed half the marina."

"That include you?"

"Yeah."

Hale waited. Calvin crossed his arms.

"He borrowed against a crab haul back in November. Said he'd square it after Christmas. Didn't."

"How much?"

"Enough to make me care."

Jonah watched his face. Calvin wasn't trying to soften himself. If anything, he looked almost irritated at being forced to explain ordinary anger to people who should already understand it.

"Did you hit him?" Hale asked.

Calvin shrugged once.

"He shoved me. I shoved back."

"That all?"

Calvin looked at Jonah briefly, as if only just now realizing there was a teenager standing in the middle of this conversation.

"Why's he here?"

Hale didn't answer that. He just said, "Did you hit him?"

Calvin looked back at the detective.

"No."

Jonah studied him. The answer wasn't clean. Not because it was definitely false. Because it came with the faint jagged edge of selective memory. Maybe no punch. Maybe enough force to count as one depending on whose version you took.

Hale asked, "When'd you last see him?"

"After he walked off."

"Toward where?"

"The lot. Same as everybody else."

"Did he seem drunk?"

Calvin snorted.

"When didn't Josh seem at least halfway on the road there?"

Not a real answer. Hale seemed to know it too.

"Did you see him get into a truck? Take a boat? Talk to anyone after?"

"No."

The harbor went quiet around them for a moment except for the slap of water under the slips and the soft buzz of the office radio inside.

Then Calvin said, "You think I did something to him?"

Hale's expression didn't move.

"I think you fought with him the day he went missing."

Calvin's jaw tightened.

"That's a long walk from murder."

Nobody had said murder. Jonah felt the word strike the air between them like metal on stone. Hale did not react visibly, but Jonah saw the stillness deepen in him. Calvin seemed to realize it too, a fraction too late. He looked away toward the lot.

"Missing," he said. "Whatever."

Too fast. Too casual. Jonah felt the first real shift of the case happen right there, under the awning in the cold harbor air. Not because Calvin looked guilty. Because he looked possible. And possible was enough to change the shape of a disappearance.

Hale said quietly, "Stay in town."

Calvin gave him a hard look.

"Wasn't planning a cruise."

Then he turned and walked back through the lot toward his truck without another word. Jonah watched him go. Water dripped from the awning in a slow steady rhythm beside them.

The marina lights shimmered in the puddles at their feet. And somewhere behind them, inside the warm orderly office of Townsend Marine Repair, Derek Townsend remained exactly what he had looked like all evening. Reasonable. Helpful. Clean.

Hale looked out across the lot for a moment longer, then said, "Well."

Jonah glanced up. "That sounded promising."

"It sounded like a suspect."

Jonah looked toward Calvin's truck as it started and backed out of its space.

"Do you think it's him?"

Hale watched the taillights disappear toward the road.

"I think," he said, "that men who fight over money the day someone disappears tend to get my attention."

He turned toward the harbor.

"And I think this just stopped being simple."

The wind shifted across the marina, colder now, carrying the smell of tidewater and machinery and something deeper from beyond the breakwater. Jonah looked past the slips toward the black line of open water. The missing man. The skiff in the dark. The fight over money. The careful man in the repair shop who had told the truth quickly enough to look harmless. Somewhere inside all of it, something wasn't lining up. Jonah could feel that much already.

Chapter 5

The coffee shop on Harbor Road was warmer than it had any right to be. Not physically. Though it was warm enough, with fogged windows and the soft hiss of milk steaming somewhere behind the counter. What Jonah noticed first whenever he stepped inside was the feeling of the place. It had the kind of warmth people created on purpose. Lamps instead of bright overhead lights. Scratched wooden tables that didn't match. A shelf of used paperbacks near the window. Soft music low enough that it didn't try to compete with conversation.

In summer it filled with tourists in rain jackets asking for extra syrups and directions to the beach. In winter it belonged to Seabrook. People who knew each other. People who didn't always speak but nodded.

People who took the same corner table every Thursday without needing to discuss it. Jonah stood near the pickup counter with both hands around a paper cup Hale had handed him ten minutes earlier with the exact same expression he used when assigning simple chores to people who would rather not admit they appreciated them.

"Coffee," Hale had said. "Then you sit down and look like a civilian for five minutes."

Jonah had not pointed out that he was, in fact, a civilian. Mostly because Hale had clearly not meant it literally.

Outside, the sky had gone the same dull winter gray it had worn all week, and a fine mist drifted past the windows in slanting lines. The harbor sat somewhere beyond the row of storefronts across the street, unseen but always faintly present in the air. Salt. Wet wood. Engine oil from trucks heading in and out of the marina.

Hale sat at a small table near the back with a file folder open beside his cup, though he wasn't reading it now. He was watching the room the way he watched most places. Casually, if you didn't know him. Deliberately, if you did.

Jonah stood near the counter a moment longer, scanning the room without trying to make it obvious. The morning crowd had thinned. Two fishermen in orange bib overalls sat near the front window talking in low voices over coffee and cinnamon rolls. An older woman in a dark coat read a paperback near the shelf by the door. Someone at the far end of the room typed steadily on a laptop, earbuds in, head down.

Then the bell above the front door chimed. Jonah looked up. A woman stepped inside and paused just long enough to let the door close behind her. She wore a dark green coat damp at the shoulders from mist and carried herself with that particular kind of careful neatness some people seemed to wear like armor. Her hair was pulled back loosely, not styled so much as kept under control. She looked to be in her thirties. Maybe younger. It was always hard to tell with people who carried tension well.

For a second she just stood there, letting her eyes adjust to the warmer light. Then she moved toward the counter. Jonah felt something shift before he knew why. Not fear exactly. More like caution practiced so often it had become part of the body. He glanced toward Hale. The detective had seen her too. Not with surprise. Recognition. He closed the file folder without rushing and rose from his chair.

The woman noticed him only when he was a few steps away, and something changed in her face immediately. Not dramatically. Nothing anyone else in the room would likely have caught. Just a brief tightening at the corners of the eyes. A pause in the shoulders.

"Mrs. Townsend," Hale said.

She gave a small polite nod.

"Detective."

Her voice was soft, even. Careful. Jonah looked at her more closely now. Emily Townsend. He knew the name before Hale said it. Knew it because Seabrook was too small for the owner of Townsend Marine Repair to have a wife no one had heard of. But hearing the name in connection with the face made something settle into place. Hale gestured lightly toward the back of the shop.

"Do you have a minute?"

Emily glanced toward the register, then toward the door, then back to Hale. The movement was quick enough that most people wouldn't notice. Jonah did.

"Yes," she said.

Hale led her toward the small table near the back, and Jonah followed a few steps later with his coffee, not because anyone had told him to but because Hale hadn't told him not to. Emily noticed him then.

For the first time since entering, something in her expression softened. Only slightly. He wasn't sure why. Maybe because he was younger. Maybe because he looked like someone who belonged in a school hallway, not in an investigation. Or maybe because people often forgot to hide certain things from teenagers until too late. Hale waited until she sat before taking his chair again.

"Thanks," he said. "I won't keep you long."

Emily folded her hands loosely in front of her cup. She hadn't ordered anything yet. Jonah noticed that too. She had walked in like someone arriving at a place where she knew what she wanted, then lost track of the reason for coming inside. Hale's voice stayed calm and ordinary.

"We're still asking around about Josh Hoggins."

At the name, Emily's gaze lifted just slightly. Not confusion. Recognition.

"He's missing," Hale continued.

A very small silence opened between them. Jonah watched the news land. It didn't hit like surprise. Not exactly. More like something she had been trying not to form into words and had now been forced to hear said aloud. Emily looked down at the table.

"I didn't know that," she said.

The sentence was smooth. The feeling beneath it wasn't. Jonah sensed fear, yes, but not the kind tied directly to Josh himself. It ran on a second track alongside something else. Anticipation. As if a door she had spent days keeping shut had just shifted on its hinges.

Hale asked, "When was the last time you saw him?"

Emily hesitated only a fraction.

"At the marina. A few days ago."

"Just saw him?"

She looked toward the window for half a second. "Yes."

Not a clean lie. Something more careful than that. A line drawn where there had been more behind it. Jonah kept still.

Hale said, "Did you speak with him?"

Emily swallowed lightly.

"Maybe just hello."

Her voice had gone quieter now. Not because the coffee shop demanded it. Because certain answers seemed to make her want to take up less space. Hale rested his hands around his cup without drinking from it.

"Josh has friends at the harbor," he said. "Coworkers. People who knew his habits. We're trying to get a clear sense of who he talked to last."

Emily nodded once, but her fingers tightened slightly around the cardboard sleeve of her cup.

"I wouldn't be much help," she said.

Jonah watched her face. The fear in her wasn't guilt. It came from another direction entirely. Protectiveness. The realization was faint at first, easy to miss in all the rest of it. But once he felt it, he couldn't shake the feeling. She wasn't frightened of being caught in something. She was frightened of something reaching her.

Hale asked a few more questions, patient and non-threatening. Had Josh been by the repair shop lately? Had Derek mentioned him? Had she heard anything about the argument at the marina? At that, Emily looked up.

"Argument?"

Hale nodded. "Derek and Josh had words on Dock C the day before Josh disappeared."

There. That changed something. Not her posture exactly. Something behind it. A tightening. A rapid internal calculation.

"He told you that?" she asked.

Hale said, "He mentioned it."

Emily looked down again. The response was small, but Jonah caught it clearly: not relief, not concern. She had expected Derek to control the version of events first. And now she knew he had.

"That sounds like Josh," she said after a second.

It was the kind of sentence people used when they wanted a conflict to belong to somebody predictable. Hale let the silence breathe.

Then he said, "And Derek?"

That one took a little longer.

"Derek doesn't really argue," she said.

Jonah looked at her carefully. The words themselves sounded harmless. Almost flattering. The feeling beneath them was not. People in town said Derek was calm the way they said the tide came in. As a fact. A character trait. A strength. Emily said it as if calm were something else. Something managed. Hale seemed to hear that too, even if not in the same way Jonah did.

He asked, "He's working today?"

Emily nodded. "At the shop."

"You heading there after this?"

The question was casual enough to be mistaken for conversation. Emily still reacted to it. Her eyes flicked to the clock above the counter. Then to the door. Then back.

"In a little while," she said.

Jonah noticed her hand move unconsciously toward the cuff of her coat. She straightened it though it didn't need straightening. A tiny act. A practiced one.

Hale asked, "Did Josh ever come by the house?"

Emily's gaze sharpened, just for a second.

"No."

This one came quickly. Too quickly. Not because it was false, necessarily. Because it had been answered before the question finished settling in the room. Hale nodded as if that were enough. He didn't push harder. Not here.

The coffee shop around them went on breathing in its ordinary rhythm. Cups clinked. The steamer hissed behind the counter. Someone laughed softly near the front window. Outside, mist drifted past the glass in pale ribbons.

Emily looked less like someone being questioned than someone trying to remain composed inside a room that felt suddenly too warm. Then the door chimed again. Jonah turned. Derek Townsend stepped inside.

He had shed his work jacket for a dark wool coat that made him look more like a man coming from a meeting than from a repair shop. He paused near the entrance, eyes adjusting, and saw them almost immediately. The shift in Emily was instant. Jonah felt it like a door slamming shut.

Her shoulders tightened, but only by a fraction. Her face settled into something smoother. More neutral. The fear didn't disappear. It changed shape. Smaller. More controlled. Packed down fast. Derek crossed the room with the same steady composure he brought everywhere else.

"Detective," he said. "Didn't expect to see you here."

His gaze moved to Emily, then to Jonah, then back to Hale. He smiled slightly, the same calm polite expression Jonah had seen at the repair shop.

"Everything alright?"

Emily answered before Hale could.

"Yes."

Too quickly. Again, not the words. The speed. Jonah noticed that Derek noticed it too. Not with surprise. With familiarity.

Derek laid one hand lightly on the back of Emily's chair. The gesture would have looked affectionate to anyone not watching closely. Jonah was watching closely. Emily became even stiller.

Hale said, "Just asking a few follow-up questions."

"About Josh?" Derek asked.

"Yes."

Derek nodded as though this was exactly what a reasonable detective would be doing and exactly what a reasonable husband would interrupt politely without making into a scene.

"Anything helpful?" he asked.

The question was for Hale. But Jonah noticed Emily glance at Derek before looking back down at the table. Checking. Not permission exactly. Temperature.

Hale said, "Still sorting that out."

Derek gave a small nod and looked to Emily.

"Are you ready?"

Three words. Simple. But Jonah saw it immediately. The way Emily's hands tightened. The way she stood before she quite seemed to mean to. The way all the small visible caution she had worn when Derek wasn't there became something sharper and quieter in his presence.

Not fear of him in the obvious sense. No shrinking. No flinch. No dramatics. Just a person becoming less available to herself. Emily looked at Hale.

"I'm sorry I couldn't help more."

Her voice was perfectly polite. The line meant more than it said. Derek smiled faintly.

"She's never loved police questions," he said.

The sentence floated there, easy and social and impossible to challenge without making it something bigger. Hale rose.

"I understand."

Derek looked at Jonah then, just briefly.

"Skipping school?" he asked lightly.

Jonah met his gaze.

"Lunch break."

Derek gave the smallest amused nod, as though that settled things. Then he rested a hand very lightly at the center of Emily's back and guided her toward the door. Not pushed. Guided. Emily let him. The bell chimed once more as they stepped back out into the mist.

Only after the door shut did Jonah realize he'd been holding his coffee cup too tightly. Hale sat again without speaking. Jonah remained standing another second, looking at the glass where the last damp outline of their exit still faded.

"What?" Hale asked finally.

Jonah sat down slowly.

"She changed."

Hale looked at him.

"When he walked in."

The detective said nothing. Jonah searched for the right words.

"She wasn't comfortable before," he said. "But when it was just you asking questions, it was... different."

"How?"

Jonah glanced toward the door.

"She was scared someone might find out what she knew." He hesitated. "Then Derek came in and it became something else."

Hale's eyes stayed on him.

"Something else how?"

Jonah looked down at the table, then back up.

"Like she started measuring every word."

The detective leaned back slightly.

"You think she knows something."

"Yes."

"About Josh?"

Jonah hesitated again.

"Yes. But not just that."

Hale waited.

Jonah said, "She's protecting someone."

It took him a second to hear how strange that sounded outside his own head. But it was still the closest thing to true. Hale watched him for another moment, expression unreadable.

"Derek?"

Jonah thought back through the conversation. The way Emily had reacted to Josh's name. The way she had reacted to the argument. The way Derek's presence changed the room around her.

"No," Jonah said quietly.

That landed differently. Hale's brow shifted almost imperceptibly.

"No?"

Jonah shook his head. "Not Derek."

The detective was silent.

Then: "Who?"

Jonah looked toward the used-paperback shelf by the window. At first he thought it was just the question itself that he couldn't answer. Then he realized it was something smaller. A memory from thirty seconds earlier, surfacing late.

When Hale had asked if Josh ever came by the house, Emily had answered no too fast. And before that, when Derek mentioned the argument, she had asked: He told you that? Not What argument? Not confusion. Recognition. There had been some connection there already. Some thread. He looked back at Hale.

"I don't know yet," he said. "But she wasn't scared for Derek."

That was the part that mattered. The detective considered this quietly. Then he reached for his coffee and took the first sip Jonah had seen him take since Emily sat down.

Near the counter, the barista called out an order for a caramel latte and someone answered, "That's me," from the front table.

The room was warm again. Ordinary again. But Jonah couldn't get the feeling of Emily's shift out of his head.

Hale said, "You notice things fast."

Jonah gave him a look. "That's not exactly news."

"No." Hale set down the cup. "But being right fast and knowing why you're right are different things."

Jonah knew that. He hated that. Because sometimes what he noticed came to him whole, like weather rolling in. The shape of it before the evidence. The emotional architecture before the blueprint. And then he had to wait for the rest of the world to catch up. Hale watched the door.

"You catch anything else?"

Jonah thought.

Then: "She was going to help us more before he came in."

Hale glanced at him.

"You sure?"

Jonah nodded once.

"Not much. But something."

The detective didn't answer immediately.

Finally he said, "That's enough for now."

They left a few minutes later. The mist had thickened again, softening the edges of Harbor Road and blurring the harbor lights farther down the block. As they stepped outside, Jonah glanced automatically toward the repair shop direction, though they couldn't see it from here.

Cars moved past with headlights on. People hurried beneath umbrellas. The whole town looked like it was trying to fold itself inward against the weather.

They walked in silence for half a block before Hale said, "He came in too quickly."

Jonah looked over. Hale kept his eyes ahead.

"Derek," he said. "For a man who was supposedly just picking up coffee, he wasn't surprised to find her there."

Jonah thought about that. No, Derek hadn't looked surprised. Not really. He had looked like someone arriving where he had intended to arrive. The thought settled coldly.

"He knew she was there."

"Maybe."

"But not for sure?"

Hale shrugged slightly. "That's the problem with maybe. It likes to dress like certainty when you're tired."

They kept walking. At the corner near the florist, Hale stopped under the awning and glanced back toward the coffee shop windows, now glowing gold against the mist.

Then he said, "One more thing."

Jonah waited.

"You were right about Josh."

"About what?"

The detective looked down the road toward the harbor.

"He mattered to her."

The sentence stayed with Jonah all the way back to the bluff house. Not because it solved anything. Because it changed Josh.

Until now, Josh Hoggins had mostly existed in other people's descriptions. Loud. Unreliable. Rough around the edges. Easy to dismiss. Easy to explain. But Emily Townsend's fear when she heard he was missing had not been the fear people felt for nuisances. It had been personal. Quietly personal. And personal meant connection.

That night the ocean below Hale's house was rough enough to hear from inside. Jonah stood near the back window of the upstairs hallway looking out over the dark line of the cliffs while wind pressed rain lightly against the glass. Somewhere out there, beyond the harbor and the breakwater and the low winter clouds, the Pacific kept moving whether Seabrook slept or not.

Behind him, the house was mostly quiet. A lamp glowed in the downstairs living room. Hale's footsteps crossed once from kitchen to den, then stopped. Jonah stayed where he was. He kept seeing Emily in the coffee shop. Careful before Derek arrived. Different after.

And beneath all of it, the thing that bothered him most was not what she had hidden. It was who she had hidden it for. Not Derek. Josh. Somewhere inside that difference, the case had shifted again. And for the first time since Josh Hoggins disappeared, Jonah had the uneasy sense that the town wasn't just ignoring a missing man. It was circling something much quieter. And much worse.

Chapter 6

The ocean was louder that morning. Jonah noticed it before he even opened his eyes. The bluff house sat high enough above the cliffs that the sound of the waves usually came through the walls as a distant rhythm. Something steady and familiar. Like wind moving through trees. Today it sounded heavier.

Storm waves rolled in from the Pacific during the night, and now they broke against the rocks below in long hollow crashes that carried up through the fog and into the quiet rooms of the house. Jonah lay still for a moment listening. Then the phone rang downstairs. Once. Twice. By the third ring he could hear Hale's footsteps crossing the kitchen floor. Jonah sat up, pulled on a sweatshirt, and stepped into the hallway just as Hale answered.

"Yeah."

A pause. Jonah leaned against the upstairs railing, listening without meaning to.

"Where?" Hale said.

Another pause. Jonah could hear the ocean again in the silence between words.

"Alright," Hale said finally. "We're on the way."

He hung up. For a moment he just stood there with the phone still in his hand. Then he looked up the stairs.

"You're awake."

Jonah came down the last few steps.

"What happened?"

"Marina."

"Josh?"

Hale grabbed his jacket from the back of a chair.

"Maybe."

That was all he said. The harbor looked colder than the day before. Gray clouds hung low over the water, and a steady wind had pushed a thin line of foam against the inside of the breakwater. The docks creaked harder in their slips now, ropes pulling tight and loosening again as the tide shifted beneath them.

Jonah and Hale crossed the marina lot quickly. Pete Landry stood near the harbor office with two other dock workers, hands stuffed deep in his coat pockets. His beard was damp with mist.

"You hear yet?" Pete asked as they approached.

"Hear what?" Hale said.

Pete jerked his thumb toward Dock B.

"Calvin."

Jonah felt the shape of the morning change immediately.

"What about him?" Hale asked.

Pete exhaled.

"Someone found blood on the dock where those two fought."

The wind carried the words out across the harbor. Jonah glanced toward the slips. Dock B stretched out into the gray water, empty except for a small work skiff rocking against its lines.

"Fresh?" Hale asked.

Pete shrugged.

"Hard to say. Rain washed most of it."

Jonah and Hale walked down the dock together. The wood was slick beneath their boots. Halfway down the row of pilings, Hale slowed and crouched. Jonah saw it then. A dark stain worked into the grain of the boards near the edge of the dock. Not large. Not dramatic. But unmistakable once you knew what you were looking at. Blood. The wind pushed cold air across the water.

"Someone tried to scrub it," Hale said quietly.

Jonah looked closer. The boards were damp in a different pattern there. Cleaner in places.

"Calvin?" Jonah asked.

"Maybe."

Hale stood.

"But that doesn't tell us who it belonged to."

Behind them, footsteps approached along the dock. A man Jonah recognized vaguely from the marina came up carrying a coil of rope over one shoulder.

"Morning," he said to Hale.

"Morning," Hale replied.

The man looked at the stain on the dock and shook his head.

"Whole place talking about that already."

"You see anything yesterday?" Hale asked.

The man shifted the rope.

"Just heard yelling. Same as everyone."

He hesitated, then added something else.

"Josh didn't deserve that."

Jonah looked at him. The man shrugged.

"I know people say he was a pain in the neck. Sometimes he was. But he helped me last winter when my engine froze up and I couldn't afford the repair."

"Helped how?" Hale asked.

"Worked the thing apart himself. Took half a day." The man gave a small laugh. "Didn't even charge me. Said I could buy him a beer sometime."

That didn't sound like the version of Josh the harbor liked to repeat. The man adjusted the rope again.

"He wasn't as bad as people make him out to be," he said.

Then he continued down the dock.

Jonah watched him go.

"That's the first good thing anyone's said about him," he murmured.

Hale nodded.

"People are complicated."

Jonah looked back at the dark stain.

"So is this."

Calvin Rudd was already waiting near the harbor office when they returned. He stood beside his truck with both arms crossed and the same irritated expression he had worn the night before. The wind tugged at his coat as he watched Hale approach.

"You gonna ask again if I killed him?" Calvin said.

Hale stopped a few feet away.

"Where were you Thursday night?"

"Home."

"Anyone see you?"

"My brother."
"Anyone else?"
Calvin's jaw tightened.
"No."
Hale nodded slightly.
"We found blood on the dock where you and Josh fought."
Calvin didn't look surprised.
"Yeah," he said. "That's probably his."
"Probably?"
"He split his lip when he hit the railing."
Jonah watched his face carefully.
"Did you throw him into it?" Hale asked.
Calvin's irritation sharpened.
"He shoved me first."
"That wasn't the question."
Calvin exhaled sharply.
"Yes," he said.
The admission hung there between them.
"You left him standing?" Hale asked.
"Yes."
"You're sure."
Calvin looked at him with open frustration.
"Detective, if I'd killed the guy I probably wouldn't still be standing here waiting for you."
That was not unreasonable. Hale studied him a moment longer. Then he nodded once.
"Stay available."
Calvin snorted.
"Like I've got somewhere else to be."
He climbed back into his truck and drove out of the lot. Jonah watched the taillights disappear down Harbor Road.
"He looks worse now," Jonah said.
Hale nodded.
"Yeah."
"But..."
Jonah hesitated.

"But what?" Hale asked.

"Something still feels off."

Hale glanced at him.

"That's because we're still missing the center of the story."

Jonah looked back toward the water.

"Josh."

"Exactly."

Late morning drifted slowly over the marina. The wind eased a little, but the sky remained low and heavy. Fishing boats rocked quietly in their slips, their hulls creaking softly as the tide continued to move beneath them.

Jonah wandered near the fuel dock while Hale spoke with Pete inside the harbor office. He had always liked watching the boats here. Each one had its own personality. Different engines. Different wear patterns. Different smells of oil and salt.

Near the edge of the dock sat a small metal cabinet mounted to the railing. Fuel logs. Boat owners recorded usage there when they filled tanks after hours. Jonah flipped the binder open absently.

The pages were damp at the edges from the mist. Names. Boat numbers. Gallons used. Most entries looked normal. Then something caught his eye. He leaned closer. One line near the bottom of the page had been written late the previous night. The handwriting looked hurried.

Boat: Sea Mist

Fuel: 18 gallons

Time: 11:40 PM

Jonah frowned. He knew the Sea Mist. Everyone at the marina did. It belonged to Derek Townsend. And Derek had told Hale he left the repair shop around eight. Jonah stared at the entry a moment longer. Eighteen gallons was enough fuel to go a long way in a skiff. Out past the harbor. Out past the islands. The wind rattled the pages of the binder. Jonah closed it slowly. Inside the harbor office, Pete was still talking.

"...and then Calvin storms off again like always," Pete said through the open door. "Guy's got two settings. Mad and madder."

Jonah stepped inside.

"Hale."

The detective looked up.

"What is it?"

Jonah held up the binder.

"Something weird in the fuel log."

Hale walked over. Jonah pointed to the entry. Hale read it once. Then again.

"The Sea Mist," he said quietly.

Jonah nodded.

"And Derek said he went home at eight."

Pete leaned over their shoulders.

"That's Townsend's boat," he said.

The harbor office went quiet for a moment. Outside, a gull cried somewhere over the water. Hale closed the binder.

"Maybe someone borrowed it."

"Maybe," Jonah said.

But neither of them sounded convinced. They stepped back outside. The harbor stretched gray and restless under the winter sky. Jonah leaned against the railing. Something about the morning felt heavier now. Not clearer. Just more complicated. Behind them, Pete came out of the office again.

"Oh," he said suddenly. "I almost forgot."

Hale looked back.

"What?"

Pete scratched his beard.

"One of the deckhands mentioned something earlier."

"What kind of something?" Hale asked.

Pete shrugged.

"Said Josh had been helping someone lately."

Jonah felt the world narrow slightly.

"Helping who?" Hale said.

Pete shook his head.

"That's the weird part."

He looked out across the harbor.

"Apparently he wouldn't say."

The wind moved softly across the water. Jonah thought about Emily in the coffee shop. The way she had reacted when she heard Josh was missing. The fear. The protectiveness. The careful answers. And the way everything about her had changed the moment Derek walked through the door. Jonah looked back at Hale.

"I think I know who."

The detective studied him carefully.

"Yeah?"

Jonah nodded slowly.

"I think Josh was helping Emily Townsend."

The harbor creaked quietly around them. And for the first time since the investigation began, the pieces of the story began sliding toward something darker than a marina fight or a drunken accident. Something hidden. Something dangerous. Something the town of Seabrook had been standing beside all along without quite seeing it.

Chapter 7

The wipers moved in a steady rhythm across Hale's windshield. Back and forth. The rain had started again ten minutes after they left the marina, not hard but persistent, the kind of Oregon coast rain that seemed less like weather and more like atmosphere deciding to settle lower.

Jonah sat in the passenger seat watching Harbor Road slide past in wet gray streaks. Storefront windows glowed faintly in the early evening. A pair of gulls stood in the middle of an empty intersection until Hale's truck got close enough to force them into the air with annoyed flaps of white wings. Neither of them had said much for the first few minutes. The fuel log sat between them now like a third person in the cab.

Sea Mist

11:40 PM

18 gallons

Derek's boat. Derek's timeline. A gap where something had happened. Hale turned onto a narrower residential street lined with dark hedges and older houses with porches pulled close against the weather.

"You're very quiet," he said.

Jonah kept looking out the window.

"That's usually my thing."

"Not this quiet."

Jonah let that sit for a second.

"You think I'm wrong."

Hale glanced at him briefly, then back at the road.

"No."

"About Emily."

"I think," Hale said carefully, "that you noticed something real."

Jonah looked over.

"But?"

Hale exhaled softly through his nose.

"But noticing a connection and proving one are different jobs."

That was fair. Annoying, but fair. Rain ticked against the glass. Jonah looked back toward the street ahead. The houses here sat a little farther apart than the ones near the harbor, nicer but not showy. The kind of neighborhood people in Seabrook described as "stable" when they wanted to mean respectable and didn't care how it sounded.

"Do you think Derek took the boat out?" Jonah asked.

Hale's hands stayed loose on the wheel.

"I think someone did."

"That's not an answer."

"It's the only honest one I've got."

Jonah leaned his head lightly against the cold window glass. The truck slowed at a stop sign.

"Why would Josh help her?" Hale asked.

Jonah frowned slightly. "You're asking me?"

"I'm asking what you think."

Jonah thought back to the coffee shop. Emily's face when she heard Josh was missing. The protective fear in it. Not grief. Not exactly. Something caught midway between dread and loyalty.

"Maybe because someone had to," Jonah said.

Hale didn't respond that right away. Outside, rain slicked the pavement black beneath the streetlights.

Finally he said, "That's not usually enough."

Jonah turned his head.

"For you?"

"For most people."

That landed harder than Jonah expected. Maybe because it was true. People noticed things. They noticed too much sometimes. Bruises explained away. Silence at the wrong moments. The way a person changed when someone else entered the room. But noticing and stepping in were very different things. The truck turned again.

At the far end of the block stood a small neighborhood market with a pharmacy counter and a narrow overhang above the side-walk. A few people moved in and out beneath umbrellas. Then Jonah saw her.

"Slow down."

Hale eased off the gas immediately.

"What?"

Jonah leaned forward slightly.

"There."

Under the awning near the market entrance, Emily Townsend stood with a grocery bag tucked against one hip and her coat collar lifted against the rain. She looked smaller out here than she had in the coffee shop. Less composed. Maybe because she was alone. Or thought she was. Hale pulled into a space across the street and cut the engine. Rain whispered across the roof.

"You want to talk to her?" he asked.

Jonah was already reaching for the door handle.

"You're not official enough for that to be a good idea," Hale said.

Jonah paused. Then Hale sighed.

"Which means I'm assuming you're going anyway."

Jonah glanced at him.

"You coming?"

"Not yet."

That made sense too. Hale in the background meant Emily might say more. Jonah stepped out into the rain. The cold hit him immediately, sharp and damp and smelling faintly of cedar mulch from the planter boxes outside the market. He crossed the street under the weak protection of his hood and reached the awning just as Emily started toward the curb. She saw him and stopped. For one quick second alarm flashed across her face. Then recog-nition replaced it.

"Jonah," she said.

Her voice was softer here than in the coffee shop. Less mea-sured, at least at first.

"Hi."

He stopped a few feet away, not crowding her.

"Sorry," he said. "I didn't mean to startle you."

Emily shook her head once.

"It's alright."

Rain dripped steadily from the edge of the awning between them. Cars moved past in a blur of headlights and spray. For a moment neither of them said anything. Then Emily looked past him toward the truck across the street.

"Hale's with you."

It wasn't a question.

Jonah nodded once. "Yeah."

Something small closed in her expression. Not panic. Just caution returning to its post.

"I'm not here to ask you anything," Jonah said.

Emily gave the faintest almost-smile.

"That's funny."

Jonah blinked. "Why?"

"Because that's exactly what people say before they ask something."

He almost smiled back.

"Fair."

Emily shifted the grocery bag slightly in her arms. Jonah noticed her knuckles were pale where she gripped the paper handles. She looked tired. Not sleepy. Worn. The kind of tired that settled behind the eyes after too many days of being alert.

Jonah said, "You were different at the coffee shop."

The words came out more directly than he meant them to. Emily's gaze lifted.

"Different?"

"When Derek came in."

The change in her was immediate again, though smaller this time. Not because Derek was here. Because his name was. She looked down at the bag in her arms.

"People act differently around their husbands all the time," she said.

The sentence was smooth. The fear beneath it wasn't. Jonah

stood still.

"I wasn't talking about normal."

Emily swallowed lightly. The rain kept falling around them, making the whole little awning feel separate from the rest of the street. She looked toward the road again.

Then quietly, "You shouldn't be involved in this."

Jonah didn't answer right away.

Finally he said, "Josh mattered to you."

Her face changed before she could stop it. There it was again. It wasn't romance or grief exactly, but awareness that had no safe place to go now that the name had been spoken aloud too many times. Emily closed her eyes for one second, then opened them.

"He was kind to me," she said.

That was all. But the sentence held far more than it appeared to. Jonah felt it immediately. Not the full story. Just the shape of one. Kindness given quietly. Kindness remembered carefully. Kindness dangerous enough that even saying that much had cost her something. Emily looked down the street behind her, toward where her house must have been. Then back to Jonah.

"If Detective Hale asks," she said, "I didn't tell you anything."

Her voice was still calm. But underneath it sat something sharper now. Fear, yes. And urgency.

Jonah said, "Emily..."

She shook her head once.

"No."

The word was small but final. Then she stepped away from the awning into the rain and hurried down the block, grocery bag held tight to her coat. Jonah watched her go until she disappeared behind a line of hedges and wet parked cars. When he got back into the truck, Hale looked at him once and started the engine.

"Well?"

Jonah shut the door.

"She said Josh was kind to her."

Hale's hands paused very briefly on the steering wheel.

"That's all?"

"No." Jonah looked back through the rain-streaked rear window, though Emily was gone now. "It's not all. It's just all she said."

Hale pulled away from the curb.

"And?"

Jonah thought of the way Emily had said kind. Like it was both a truth and a risk.

"She's scared."

"Him?"

Jonah looked over. "Derek?"

Hale nodded. Jonah watched the wipers push rain aside again.

"Yes," he said. Then, after a beat: "But not in the way people think."

Hale glanced at him.

"What does that mean?"

Jonah looked down at his hands.

"It means she's not scared he'll yell."

That was all he could explain cleanly. And even that felt heavier once said aloud. They drove the rest of the way to the marina mostly in silence. Josh's truck still sat where it had that morning.

Rain collected along the edges of the windshield and slid slowly down the glass. The blue paint looked darker in the fading light, and the whole vehicle had begun to take on that abandoned quality that developed quickly in small towns when everyone knew they belonged to someone missing. Pete Landry met them near the lot.

"Tow company's asking if they should leave it," he said.

"For now," Hale replied.

Pete nodded and lowered his voice a little.

"I found the spare key in the office drawer. Josh left it there last month after locking himself out twice in one week."

He handed Hale a small tagged keyring. Jonah looked at the truck. The paper grocery bag Emily had carried flashed unexpectedly into his mind. Then the way she had gripped it. Then the quick fear in her face when Derek's name entered the conversation. **Josh was kind to me.**

Hale unlocked the driver's side door. The smell inside the truck hit immediately. Old coffee. Damp fabric. Engine grease.

Cigarettes smoked with the windows cracked in bad weather. Josh's life, compressed into a cab.

Hale leaned in first, scanning the front seat and dashboard without touching anything. Jonah moved around to the passenger side and looked through the glass. Receipts. Loose change. A flashlight with dead batteries. A tackle magazine folded open beneath a fast-food napkin. Normal clutter. Hale opened the passenger door too.

"Gloves," he said.

Hale pulled a pair from his jacket pocket. The detective handed Jonah one set. They worked carefully. Methodically. Not because the truck had suddenly become a formal crime scene. Not yet. But because once you found one thing, you couldn't unfingerprint it.

Hale checked the glove compartment. Registration. Insurance card. A wrench. Nothing useful. Jonah looked behind the seats. A duffel bag sat shoved into the narrow space. Wet at the bottom from old boots. He pulled it out and set it on the passenger seat.

Inside were work clothes, a hoodie, a cracked phone charger, two protein bars, and a folded map of the local coastline. The map caught his attention immediately. It had been opened and refolded too many times to sit flat anymore. Jonah spread it carefully across the seat.

Several places along the shoreline had been circled in blue pen. Harbor mouth. Breakwater. The outer crab lanes. And farther out, just beyond the usual marina traffic routes, a cluster of small islands marked only by names and contour lines. One of them had a tiny X beside it. Jonah stared.

"What?" Hale asked from the driver's side.

Jonah held up the map. The detective came around. Rain tapped steadily on the truck roof above them as Hale leaned in and looked at the circled markings.

"Interesting."

Jonah's finger hovered over the X. One of the nearer islands. Small. Mostly rock and scrub by the look of it. The kind of place most people passed without much thought unless they had a reason to know it better.

"Could be fishing marks," Hale said.

"Maybe."

But Jonah didn't think so. Fishing marks weren't usually drawn like this. These circles felt purposeful. Sequential almost. Like a route being thought through rather than a location being remembered. Hale turned the map slightly.

"What else?"

Jonah looked back into the duffel. At the bottom sat a small zippered pouch. Cheap nylon, dark blue. He opened it. Inside were three things. A set of spare keys. A folded stack of cash. And a note. The note was written on the back of a torn receipt in hurried block letters.

Wait until he leaves. Light off if late. Use the side door.

No name. No signature. Just instructions. Jonah felt the world narrow around the truck cab. Hale took the note carefully and read it once. Then again. The rain outside seemed louder all at once.

"Side door to what?" Jonah asked quietly.

Hale didn't answer. Because he didn't know either. The detective looked back at the map on the seat. Then at the spare cash. Then at the note in his gloved hand.

"This wasn't random," Jonah said.

"No."

"He was planning something."

Hale nodded once.

"Yeah."

Jonah thought about Emily again. **Josh was kind to me.** The fear. The caution. The route on the map. The instructions. Wait until he leaves. Not if he leaves. Until. That sounded like planning around someone's routine. Someone watched carefully. Someone avoided. Someone dangerous enough to require doors, lights, timing.

"Emily," Jonah said.

Hale looked at him. Jonah felt the pieces moving together, not fully but enough to hear them click.

"She was leaving him."

It wasn't proof. Not yet. But it felt closer to truth than anything they had had all week. Hale folded the note back along its old crease.

"Maybe."

Jonah looked at the marked island again. The X sat there quietly in blue ink, no larger than a thumbnail. A destination. Or a meeting point. Or just a place Josh thought mattered enough to keep circling back to.

The wind rose briefly outside, rocking the truck on its springs. Somewhere across the marina a loose halyard began striking metal in sharp irregular taps. Hale looked out through the rain toward the dark shape of the harbor beyond the lot. Then back at the map. Then at Jonah.

"She frightened?" he asked.

The question took Jonah half a second to place.

"Emily?"

Hale nodded. Jonah thought back to her under the market awning. The way she had said kind. The way she had said you shouldn't be involved in this. The way urgency had hidden beneath her caution like a wire under cloth.

"Yes," Jonah said.

Hale watched him a moment longer.

"Of him?"

Jonah looked down at the note in Hale's hand. **Wait until he leaves. Light off if late.** Use the side door. That wasn't the language of argument. It was the language of escape.

"Yes," Jonah said quietly.

The detective closed the truck door slowly. Rain slid down the glass, blurring the interior again into clutter and shadow. The map, the cash, the note. A plan left unfinished. Somewhere out past the breakwater, the ocean moved in darkness toward the shore. And for the first time, the case no longer felt like a disappearance with possible violence around it. It felt like violence had always been there. Quiet. Contained.

Waiting inside a respectable house on a decent street while the town of Seabrook nodded politely and kept walking. Hale slipped the note into an evidence sleeve from his pocket.

"We do this carefully," he said.

Jonah looked toward the harbor, where the lights along the slips shimmered in the rain like small broken lines.

"Because of Derek?"

Hale's expression stayed unreadable.

"Because if Emily was trying to leave," he said, "then the moment the man stopping her thinks we know that..."

He let the sentence hang. He didn't need to finish it. Jonah already understood. The rain kept falling. The truck sat silent in the lot. And somewhere inside the dark shape of Seabrook, fear had just become visible enough to name.

Chapter 8

The next morning the fog came in before sunrise. By the time Jonah stepped into the kitchen at Hale's bluff house, the windows above the sink had turned into pale gray panels with no clear world beyond them. The ocean was still there. He could hear it beneath the fog, waves breaking below the cliffs in slow heavy crashes. But from inside the house, the Pacific might as well have been a story someone was telling from another room.

Hale stood at the counter in shirtsleeves pouring coffee into a travel mug. The yellow light over the stove cast a dull warmth across the kitchen, catching on the evidence sleeve lying flat beside the sugar bowl. Inside it, Josh's note looked smaller than it had in the truck. Harmless, almost. A scrap of paper. A few hurried lines. Nothing that should have been heavy enough to tilt a case. But it had.

Wait until he leaves. Light off if late. Use the side door.

Jonah had read it enough times last night that the words no longer arrived in sequence. They came all at once now. Like weather. Like a tone of voice. Like something coded not in secrecy but in habit. Hale screwed the lid onto the travel mug and looked up.

"You sleep?"

Jonah leaned against the doorway.

"Some."

Hale nodded toward the note. "You dream about it?"

Jonah glanced at the sleeve.

"Not exactly."

That was true. He hadn't dreamed about the note itself. He had dreamed about doors. Side doors. Back doors. Doors that didn't close all the way unless you lifted them slightly first. Houses quiet except for one room with the light still on. He hadn't said any of that out loud because saying dreams out loud often made them sound less useful than they felt. Hale picked up the evidence sleeve and slid it into a folder.

"Pete called," he said.

Jonah straightened slightly. "About what?"

"Calvin."

That sharpened the room immediately.

Hale went on, "He came back to the marina after we left."

"Why?"

"Said he remembered something."

Jonah watched him.

"Do you think that means he actually remembered something?"

Hale grabbed his keys from the counter.

"I think it means he waited all night deciding whether talking helped him more than staying quiet."

The fog pressed softly at the kitchen windows. Jonah looked toward the back porch doors where nothing but pale gray waited beyond the glass.

"So we're going back."

"Yeah."

Hale opened a drawer, pulled out another pair of gloves, and shoved them into his coat pocket.

"We're going back."

Seabrook looked half-erased in the fog. Harbor Road blurred at the edges. Storefronts appeared and disappeared in soft gray layers as Hale's truck moved through town. Brake lights ahead floated like dim red coins suspended in mist. The marina itself did not fully appear until they turned into the lot and the shapes of masts and cranes materialized all at once out of whiteness.

Everything sounded muffled. Engines. Voices. Gulls. Even the harbor seemed quieter beneath the fog, its usual slap against pilings softened into something flatter and more secretive.

Calvin waited under the awning beside the harbor office with both hands shoved into the pockets of his coat and a knit cap pulled low over his ears. He looked like he hadn't slept much either. When Hale and Jonah approached, Calvin glanced at Jonah first.

"You bring him everywhere now?"

Hale didn't answer that.

"You said you remembered something."

Calvin shifted his weight and looked out toward the slips rather than directly at either of them.

"Yeah."

He let the word hang there, as if trying to decide whether he still wanted it once it had been spoken. Pete Landry opened the harbor office door behind them.

"Coffee's on," he muttered to no one in particular, then disappeared back inside.

Hale stayed where he was.

"What did you remember?"

Calvin rubbed one hand over his beard.

"The fight wasn't just about money."

Jonah watched his face. The irritation was still there. But something else had moved in beside it now. Unease. Not guilt. Not exactly. The discomfort of realizing too late that you had been standing near something worse than you understood. Hale waited. Calvin exhaled through his nose.

"Josh said something while we were yelling."

"What?"

Calvin looked down toward the wet planks beneath the awning.

"Said if people around here had any spine, somebody would've done something already."

The words stayed in the damp air a second.

Hale asked, "Done something about what?"

Calvin shook his head once.

"He didn't say."

That was not fully true. Jonah could feel it immediately. Not a full lie. A shape cut smaller than the truth. Hale seemed to catch the same edge.

"What did you think he meant?" the detective asked.

Calvin's jaw tightened.

"I thought he was drunk and trying to start moral philosophy on the dock."

"You didn't answer my question."

Calvin looked finally at Hale.

"He meant Derek."

There it was. Not dramatic. Not loud. Just placed between them like a tool on a workbench. The fog shifted behind him, thinning just enough to reveal the dark outlines of a few outer slips before closing again.

Hale said, "Why Derek?"

Calvin hesitated.

Then: "Because he said Townsend acts like he owns more than boats."

Jonah felt something colder move through the morning.

"What does that mean?" Hale asked.

Calvin gave a short humorless laugh.

"You tell me. Josh wasn't exactly handing out footnotes."

"Did he say anything else?"

Calvin rubbed his thumb along the seam of his pocket.

"He told me to stay out of it."

"Out of what?"

"The whole damn thing." Calvin's voice roughened. "Said I didn't know enough to be useful and too much to be safe."

Hale's expression didn't change.

"When was this?"

"Right before he shoved me."

The detective nodded once.

"And now you're remembering."

Calvin looked irritated again, but at himself this time more than anyone else.

"Because at the time it sounded like Josh being Josh. Running his mouth like he'd suddenly become the patron saint of bad decisions."

He looked out into the fog.

"Now the guy's missing."

That part landed true. Hale let silence do some work.

Finally he asked, "Did Josh mention a place? Boat? Cabin? Anything concrete?"

Calvin frowned as if forcing his memory through mud. "No."

Then he paused. Actually paused. Jonah felt the shift in him a second before the words came.

"He did say one weird thing."

Hale's gaze sharpened. "What?"

Calvin looked toward the harbor mouth, though in this fog there was nothing to see except brighter gray.

"He said if Derek found out before the weekend, it was over."

Jonah's attention sharpened instantly.

"Over how?" Hale asked.

Calvin shook his head. "He didn't say."

"But he kept looking toward the water when he said it."

The world narrowed around that detail. Toward the water. Hale asked, "The marina?"

"Yeah."

"Any particular part?"

Calvin squinted, thinking.

"Not the slips." He gestured vaguely outward. "Out there."

Past the breakwater. Jonah thought of the map from Josh's truck. The circled shoreline. The marked island. The X. Fog beaded on the awning edge and dropped one cold tap at a time onto the railing beside them.

Hale said, "You tell anyone else this?"

"No."

"Why now?"

Calvin met his eyes.

"Because whatever Josh got himself into..." He glanced briefly toward Jonah, then back at Hale. "It wasn't just dock bullshit."

That was as close to honesty as Calvin had sounded yet. Hale nodded once.

"Stay available."

Calvin snorted softly.

"Seems to be my new hobby."

He walked off toward the lot without another word. Jonah watched him disappear into the fog, his broad shape thinning until it was only movement and then nothing. For a second the harbor seemed to hold its breath. Then the sounds of it returned. A forklift beeping somewhere near the fuel dock. A gull crying overhead, hidden in white. Water pushing softly at pilings you could barely see. Hale looked at Jonah.

"Well?"

Jonah kept his eyes on the fog beyond the slips.

"He's telling the truth now."

"Why?"

"Because he's scared of having been close to it."

Hale didn't argue. They stepped out from under the awning and walked toward the outer docks. The fog thickened between the slips and the harbor mouth until even the nearest working boats looked ghostly, their shapes reduced to hull lines and hanging lamps suspended in whiteness. It was the kind of weather that made distances feel wrong. The outer markers should have been visible from here. They weren't. Jonah followed Hale down the wet planks, hands in his coat pockets.

"What did Derek do this morning?" he asked.

Hale glanced at him. "What?"

"Did anyone see him?"

"Pete said he opened the shop on time."

That fit. Of course it did. Derek Townsend would open on time if the world were ending outside his office door. That was part of the problem. Reliable men made excellent shelters for terrible things.

They stopped near the end of the dock where the fog swallowed most of the channel. Hale rested one hand on the railing and looked out into the white.

"Seasonal islands sit what, fifteen, twenty minutes out in good weather?" he said.

Jonah looked at him.

"You're asking me?"

"I'm asking the person who stared at that map like it was trying to confess."

Jonah almost smiled.

"Depends on the boat."

"The Sea Mist?"

Jonah thought about the entry in the fuel log. Eighteen gallons.

"Longer out and back if he took a wide line," he said. "Less if he knew where he was going."

Hale nodded once, as if that lined up with something he was already measuring internally. The fog rolled and shifted. For just one second, a dark shape appeared farther out, low and rocky, then vanished again. An island. Or maybe just a trick of distance and weather.

Jonah said, "You thinking about the cabins."

Hale didn't answer right away. That was answer enough. A worker approached from behind carrying a coil of hose over one shoulder. Jonah recognized him as the same man who had spoken up for Josh yesterday about the frozen engine. He slowed when he saw them.

"You hear?" he asked Hale.

"Hear what?"

The man shifted the hose.

"Townsend had Danny Mercer scrub the Sea Mist this morning before sunrise."

That landed hard and quietly both.

Hale looked at him. "Scrub what?"

"Whole damn deck, according to Danny." The man frowned. "Didn't make much sense. Boat wasn't due out. Weather's been garbage. Nobody pressure-washes a skiff in this kind of fog unless they've got a reason."

Jonah felt the case tilt a little further.

"Where's Danny now?" Hale asked.

"Back in the repair bay, probably."

Hale thanked him and they turned back toward shore immediately.

As they walked, Jonah said, "That's not normal."

"No."

"He cleaned it."

"Maybe."

Jonah looked ahead through the fog where the repair sheds waited somewhere beyond the lot.

"You don't sound convinced."

Hale's boots struck the planks in a quick steady rhythm.

"Because too clean can mean too many things."

"But it still means too clean."

That got the smallest corner of a smile out of Hale.

"Yeah."

They found Danny Mercer in Townsend Marine's side bay, hosing grime from an outboard housing that didn't seem especially interested in becoming cleaner. He looked younger than Jonah expected, maybe mid-twenties, with red hands and the permanently damp expression of someone who spent too much time working around cold water. He looked up when Hale entered.

"Detective."

"Danny."

Hale stopped a few feet away.

"You cleaned the Sea Mist this morning."

Danny glanced instinctively toward the office door before answering. Jonah noticed that immediately.

"Yeah."

"Why?"

"Derek asked me to."

"What for?"

Danny shrugged.

"Said it was overdue."

Hale let that hang.

"In weather like this?"

Another glance toward the office. Danny lowered the hose nozzle.

"There was mud on the deck," he said.

That sharpened the room.

"Mud?" Hale asked.

Danny nodded.

"Not a lot. Just enough that he wanted it gone before customers came around."

Jonah watched him carefully. There was nervousness there now. Not deep. Not criminal. Just the unease of a man realizing a routine work task might not have been routine at all.

"Where on the deck?" Hale asked.

"Near the stern. Some on the side rail."

Danny swallowed.

"Looked like marsh mud. Not harbor stuff."

The words hung in the oily air of the repair bay. Marsh mud. Not harbor. Jonah thought of the islands again. Not the rocky ones the ferries passed sometimes in summer. The lower winter islands. The ones with reeds and narrow docks and crab sheds that sat half-abandoned off season.

The subtle thread from the map in Josh's truck tightened another notch. Hale asked a few more questions. When did Derek ask him? How early? Was Derek already there when Danny arrived? Had Derek said where the boat had been?

Seven-ish.

Yes.

No.

Useful. Not conclusive. Yet. When they stepped back outside, the fog had not lifted at all. If anything, it had settled lower, making the far side of the lot seem farther away than it was. Jonah shoved his hands deeper into his pockets.

"He's cleaning up."

Hale stood still for a second, looking not at the harbor this time but beyond it in his mind. Mapping something.

"Maybe."

"That's a lot of maybes."

"Welcome to police work."

Jonah let out a quiet breath. The wind changed. Not stronger. Colder. He looked toward the harbor mouth again, though there was nothing to see but white.

"What if Josh got there before Derek expected?" he said.

Hale glanced at him.

"To the island."

The detective didn't answer immediately.

Jonah continued, "What if the note was for Emily. What if Josh was setting up where she'd go. What if Derek found out before the weekend, like Calvin said, and that's why Josh said it would be over."

Hale's expression stayed unreadable, but Jonah could feel his attention sharpening around the idea.

"That's one theory," Hale said.

Jonah looked back toward the repair shop.

"It fits too much."

"Maybe." Hale's gaze followed his toward Townsend Marine. "But a theory that fits is still a theory."

He took out his phone, looked at the screen, then slipped it back into his pocket. Finally he said the thing Jonah had been waiting for without entirely knowing it.

"We need to start looking offshore."

The sentence seemed to change the air. Not because it solved anything. Because it committed to something. Until now the case had moved along the harbor, through parking lots and coffee shops and workbenches and truck cabs. Land-bound explanations. Town-sized explanations.

Offshore was different. Offshore meant places that didn't belong to ordinary routines. Places people only went with purpose. Jonah looked out into the blank white beyond the docks.

Somewhere out there sat the island on Josh's map. Maybe more than one. Crab cabins. Storage sheds. Narrow docks lost half the year to fog and weather and the kind of quiet that could keep a secret if no one came asking. Hale adjusted his coat against the cold.

"We do this carefully."

Jonah nodded.

"Because if we're right…"

Hale looked toward the harbor mouth one last time.

"Then we're already late."

That stayed with Jonah harder than anything else all morning. The fog. The cleaned boat. The marsh mud. The marked island. Emily's fear. Josh's note. And now that one sentence. We're already late.

The harbor had gone so quiet beneath the fog that the next gull cry sounded almost human before it broke apart in the air. Jonah stood beside Hale at the end of the dock and stared into the whiteness beyond the breakwater. For the first time since Josh Hoggins disappeared, the case no longer felt like something circling Seabrook from the outside. It felt as if it had already passed through the middle of the town, taken what it wanted, and gone somewhere small and silent to wait. And now they were going to have to follow it.

Chapter 9

By midafternoon the fog began to loosen. It didn't clear all at once. It never did on the Oregon coast. Instead it thinned in long quiet shifts, lifting off the harbor water first and then retreating slowly toward the outer channel like a curtain being drawn back by someone patient.

From the bluff above the marina, Jonah watched the change happen in pieces. First the tops of the breakwater markers appeared. Then the outlines of the outer slips sharpened. Then the gray horizon emerged, faint but solid enough that the ocean felt like a place again rather than a rumor hidden behind fog.

Hale stood beside him on the gravel turnout above the harbor, one hand resting on the roof of the truck while he spoke quietly into his phone. Jonah didn't hear most of the conversation, just the occasional words carried by the wind.

"...yes."

"...no, not yet."

"...small islands west of the crab lanes."

"...I'll take responsibility for it."

The ocean below rolled in long steel-colored lines beneath the breaking clouds. Out past the harbor mouth, darker shapes began to surface from the fog's retreat. Islands. Low. Uneven. Mostly rock and scrub. The kind of places people forgot about most of the year. Hale ended the call and slipped the phone into his pocket.

"Marine deputy's meeting us at the dock," he said.

Jonah nodded. They drove down to the marina without saying much. The harbor felt different now that the fog had lifted halfway. Boats that had been ghosts an hour earlier sat fully visible in their slips again, their rigging clinking softly in the wind. A few fishermen moved along the docks preparing gear for evening runs, their voices drifting across the water.

The Sea Mist sat where it always did beside Townsend Marine's service pier. Clean. Too clean. The hull glistened with fresh rinse water that hadn't fully dried yet. The deck rails shone faintly in the weak sunlight. If Jonah hadn't known about the mud Danny Mercer described that morning, nothing about the boat would have seemed unusual now. But knowing changed things.

Jonah slowed slightly as they walked past. The repair bay doors were open. Inside, Derek Townsend stood near a workbench speaking with another mechanic. His posture was relaxed, one hand resting casually against the counter as if the entire town had not spent the last three days talking about a missing man who had argued with him hours before disappearing.

He looked up as Hale and Jonah crossed the dock. For just a moment his eyes followed them. Not curious. Measured. The way a man might watch someone approaching a door he'd always believed belonged to him.

Then he returned to his conversation without acknowledgment. Hale didn't break stride. Jonah glanced once over his shoulder. Derek was still watching them.

The marine deputy waited beside a narrow patrol boat tied to the outer dock. His name was Hoffman, and he looked like he had spent most of his life working around water. Weathered skin. Broad shoulders. A knit cap pulled low against the wind.

"You the ones chasing islands?" he asked as Hale approached.

"That's the plan," Hale said.

Hoffman nodded toward the harbor mouth.

"Visibility's better than it was this morning. Tide's turning out though."

"That a problem?"

"Not unless you don't know where the rocks are."

Jonah stepped aboard behind them as Hoffman untied the stern line. The boat's engine rumbled to life with a low mechanical vibration that carried up through the metal deck. Hale took the passenger seat beside the console while Jonah settled onto the narrow bench behind them.

The marina slipped away quickly once they cleared the last row of docks. Wind cut colder across the open water. The breakwater rose on either side of the channel like dark walls, the rocks still wet from the morning fog. Beyond them the Pacific opened wide and restless, gray waves rolling slowly beneath the clearing sky. Hoffman angled the patrol boat west. Jonah leaned forward slightly, watching the water move past the hull.

Out here the town already felt distant. Seabrook shrank behind them into a cluster of roofs and cranes pressed against the shoreline. Ahead stretched open water broken only by scattered islands and long lines of crab pots bobbing gently in the swell. Hale glanced back at Jonah.

"You still remember that map?"

Jonah nodded.

"There were four circles."

Hoffman glanced over his shoulder.

"Fishing marks?"

"No," Jonah said. "Routes."

He pointed ahead.

"The first one was near the crab lanes."

Hoffman adjusted the throttle slightly and steered toward a cluster of orange floats drifting in a rough grid across the water. They passed them slowly. Nothing unusual. Just gear. But Jonah could feel the map in his mind, the way the circles had stepped outward from the harbor like stones in a path.

"The second one was farther west," he said.

Hoffman followed the direction. The islands grew larger ahead. Most of them were little more than uneven ridges of rock and scrub grass with gulls circling overhead. A few had narrow docks left over from old crab operations that only ran during certain months of the year. Hoffman slowed the boat.

"You looking for something specific?"

"Footprints," Hale said.

Hoffman snorted.

"On rock?"

"On mud."

That changed the deputy's expression slightly.

"There's marsh edges on a couple of these," he said.

He turned the boat toward the nearest island. The shoreline rose slowly ahead of them, jagged stone giving way to a narrow strip of darker ground near the waterline where reeds and marsh grass grew thick. Hoffman idled closer.

"Careful," he muttered. "Bottom gets shallow."

Jonah stood, gripping the rail as the patrol boat drifted along the muddy edge. At first the ground looked empty. Just wind-bent grass and dark patches of wet soil. Then Jonah saw them.

"Stop."

Hoffman eased the throttle back immediately. Jonah pointed.

"There."

Hale leaned forward. Along the narrow strip of marsh mud between grass and water sat a series of shallow impressions. Boot prints. Not old. The edges were still sharp enough to catch the light. Hoffman whistled softly.

"Someone's been here."

Jonah crouched near the rail to see better. The prints moved from the waterline toward the interior of the island where thicker brush hid the ground from view.

"Boat landed here," Hale said quietly.

Hoffman nodded.

"Mud like that would stick to a deck easy."

Jonah felt the connection tighten instantly. Marsh mud. The Sea Mist. The cleaned deck. He looked toward the interior of the island.

"Do people use cabins out here?"

Hoffman shrugged.

"Couple of them, yeah. Mostly seasonal crab shacks. Nobody stays year-round."

Jonah's eyes scanned the brush. Something sat back there. Hidden by scrub and small wind-bent trees. A shape too straight to be natural.

"Wait," Jonah said.

Hoffman followed his gaze. At first there was nothing. Then

80

the angle of the sunlight shifted through the thinning clouds, and the shape appeared. A roofline. Low. Weathered gray wood. Half-hidden among the brush like something the island itself had tried to swallow. Hoffman leaned forward.

"Well I'll be damned."

Hale didn't speak. The patrol boat drifted quietly in the water beside the marsh edge. The cabin sat about fifty yards inland, barely visible except for the corner of its roof and a narrow dock extending into a small inlet cut into the island's side. No smoke. No movement.

Just a small forgotten structure sitting alone against the wind and sea. Jonah felt something heavy settle in his chest. The map. The circles. The X. This was the place. Hale stared at the cabin for a long moment.

Then he said quietly, "We're not going in today."

Hoffman glanced at him.

"Why not?"

"Because if someone's been using it recently," Hale said, "I don't want them seeing us land."

Jonah understood immediately. If Derek had come here... And if Derek believed no one knew... They still had the advantage. Hoffman nodded slowly.

"Smart."

He eased the patrol boat into a slow turn away from the island. Jonah kept watching the cabin as it drifted farther back. From a distance it looked even smaller. Just a gray box of wood and shadow sitting quietly on a piece of land most of Seabrook probably forgot existed. But Jonah could feel it now. The weight of the place. The way the air around it seemed colder. The way the map had led directly here.

Behind them the mainland shoreline began to grow again through the clearing haze. Seabrook returning. But Jonah kept his eyes on the island until it finally disappeared behind the swell. Hale looked back at him once.

"We come back tomorrow," he said.

Jonah nodded. Because they both knew the same thing now.

Whatever had happened to Josh Hoggins... The answer was waiting in that cabin. And the ocean had already kept it hidden long enough.

Chapter 10

Dawn came slowly over the Pacific. The sky began as a pale gray seam along the horizon, the kind that barely separated ocean from air. By the time Hale and Jonah reached the marina, a faint blue light had started to spread across the water, flattening the waves into dull sheets of steel.

The harbor was almost empty. A few crab boats rocked gently in their slips. Somewhere farther down the docks a gull cried once, then went quiet again. The cold had settled deep into the morning, sharp enough that Jonah could see his breath when he exhaled. Deputy Hoffman waited beside the patrol boat, already warming the engine.

"Morning," he said quietly as they approached.

Hale nodded.

"How's the tide?"

"Dropping," Hoffman replied. "We've got a couple hours before it swings."

That was good enough. None of them said anything more as they climbed aboard. The engine rumbled low and steady as Hoffman eased the boat away from the dock. The marina lights faded behind them as they passed through the breakwater, the open Pacific waiting beyond like a darker version of the sky above it.

Jonah pulled his coat tighter against the wind. The cold offshore air always felt different. Cleaner. Sharper. Less forgiving. They rode mostly in silence. The islands emerged slowly from the gray morning the same way they had the day before, low shapes rising from the water as the light strengthened. Hoffman angled the patrol boat toward the same marsh edge they had seen the footprints along.

The shoreline looked unchanged. Reeds bending gently in the wind. Dark mud exposed by the lowering tide. And there, still pressed into the damp ground, the same line of boot prints leading inland. Hoffman cut the engine. The sudden quiet felt enormous.

"Alright," he said.

Hale stepped onto the muddy bank first, boots sinking slightly into the wet ground. Jonah followed carefully behind him, the marsh mud sucking softly at the soles of his boots. The footprints were clearer this morning. Deep enough that small pools of water had collected in the impressions overnight.

Jonah crouched for a second. They were the same prints. Same direction. Someone had come ashore here. But no one had left. Hale glanced back toward the boat.

"Stay close," he said to Hoffman.

The deputy nodded and secured the patrol boat to a half-rotted dock post. Jonah followed Hale up the narrow path where the footprints disappeared into taller grass. The island felt quieter than the ocean around it.

The wind moved through the brush with a soft dry sound. Small birds flicked between branches overhead and vanished again. The ground rose gently beneath their boots as the path wound toward the center of the island.

The cabin appeared gradually through the brush. First the roofline. Then the weathered gray walls. Then the small wooden porch facing the narrow inlet where the dock reached into the water.

Up close, the structure looked older than Jonah expected. The wood had turned nearly silver from years of salt air. One of the window shutters hung slightly crooked. The door stood closed but not fully latched. Hale slowed.

Jonah noticed something else then. The smell. It drifted faintly through the cold air. Not strong. But wrong. Something sour beneath the scent of salt and damp wood. Hale noticed it too. They stopped about fifteen feet from the cabin. Neither of them spoke. Hoffman came up quietly behind them.

"You smell that?" he asked.

Hale nodded once. The three of them stood there for a moment, listening. Nothing moved inside the cabin. No voices. No footsteps. Only the wind brushing the grass and the distant low rhythm of the ocean.

Hale approached the door slowly. He rested one hand on the wood and pushed gently. The door opened with a dry creak. The smell strengthened immediately. Jonah felt his stomach tighten.

Inside, the cabin was small. One main room. A narrow counter along one wall. A rusted stove. A wooden table with two chairs. Dust clung to most surfaces, but parts of the room looked disturbed recently. The floorboards near the center showed darker streaks where something heavy had been dragged or shifted. Jonah stepped inside behind Hale. The air inside felt stale and cold. Hoffman moved toward the small back window, scanning the room.

"Doesn't look like anyone's here now," he muttered.

Jonah's eyes moved slowly across the cabin. The table held an empty water bottle and a half-used roll of duct tape. The counter held a rusted lantern. Then he noticed the back corner of the room. At first it looked like a pile of old blankets. But the shape was wrong. Too solid. Too still. Jonah felt his chest tighten.

"Hale."

The detective turned. Jonah pointed. Hale crossed the room slowly. The blankets had been pulled halfway over a body. Josh Hoggins lay on his side against the wall. His clothes were stiff with dried blood along one shoulder. His face had taken on the pale gray tone of someone who had been dead long enough that the room itself seemed to recognize it. Hoffman inhaled sharply behind them.

"Jesus."

Hale crouched beside the body. Jonah stood a few feet away, unable to move closer. The room felt smaller now. Josh's boots were still on. Mud clung to the soles. Marsh mud. The same dark mud from the shoreline. Hale examined the wound along Josh's shoulder and neck carefully without touching anything.

"Blunt trauma," he said quietly.

"From the fight?" Hoffman asked.

Hale shook his head.

"No."

Jonah stared at the floorboards. Three days. Josh had been here three days. The water bottle on the table. The duct tape. The blankets. He had been alive when he was brought here. Left. Jonah swallowed.

"We were too late."

Hale didn't answer. Because there was nothing useful to say to that. Hoffman moved slowly around the room, scanning for anything else disturbed.

"Hale," he said after a moment.

The detective stood and joined him near the back wall. Jonah followed. Hoffman pointed toward the corner near the door. A coil of rope sat there. The same pale blue dock rope used throughout the marina. Tied into a loop. And next to it sat a small object half-hidden beneath the rope. A metal fuel cap. Stamped with the name of a boat manufacturer. Hale picked it up carefully with a gloved hand. Jonah leaned closer. He recognized it immediately.

"Sea Mist."

The name was engraved into the underside of the cap. Hoffman let out a slow breath.

"That's not subtle."

Hale stared at the cap for a moment. Then he slipped it into an evidence bag. Outside the cabin the wind moved through the grass again. The ocean continued its endless slow breathing beyond the island.

Jonah looked back toward Josh's body. Three days. Maybe longer. Left alone in a cold cabin while the town argued about drunken accidents and dock fights. Left to die. Hale stepped toward the doorway.

He stood there looking out across the small inlet where the patrol boat waited quietly against the dock. Then he turned back to Jonah. His voice was calm. But something inside it had hardened.

"We're done asking questions," he said.

Jonah understood. Back in Seabrook, Derek Townsend was

probably already at work in his repair shop. Opening the doors. Greeting customers. Acting like a man who owned his place in the world. Hale stepped out into the morning wind.

"Let's go arrest him."

Chapter 11

The patrol boat cut through the gray water on the return trip, its engine steady and low against the wind. No one spoke much. Hoffman stood at the console, eyes on the channel markers ahead. Hale sat beside him with his coat collar pulled up against the cold. Jonah remained on the rear bench where he had sat on the way out, watching the island slowly shrink behind them.

From this distance it looked harmless. Just another low shape of rock and scrub grass rising from the Pacific. A place you could pass a hundred times without noticing. Jonah kept thinking about the cabin. The blankets. The water bottle on the table. Josh Hoggins had been alive when he was brought there. That part had settled into Jonah's chest like cold metal. Alive. And alone.

The boat crossed the breakwater and the marina came into view again, rows of slips and masts stretching along the harbor like a small floating city waking into the morning. The sky had brightened slightly since they left, but the light remained flat and colorless, the kind that made every shadow feel heavier than it should. Hoffman slowed the patrol boat as they approached the dock. Hale stood before the engine even fully idled.

"We go straight there," he said.

Hoffman nodded. Jonah stepped onto the dock behind Hale as the patrol boat bumped softly against the rubber fenders. The marina already felt different. Word had begun to move through town the way it always did in places like Seabrook. Not loudly. Not yet. But something in the air had shifted.

A few dock workers paused as Hale passed them. Pete Landry stood outside the harbor office holding a mug of coffee. His expression changed immediately when he saw Hale's face.

"You found him," Pete said quietly.

Hale nodded once. Pete looked down at the boards for a moment.

"Damn."

Then he stepped aside without another word. Jonah and Hale walked the length of the dock toward Townsend Marine. The Sea Mist sat exactly where it had the day before. Still clean. Still quiet.

The repair bay doors were open again. Inside, Derek Townsend stood at a workbench with a clipboard in one hand and a wrench in the other. A radio played softly somewhere in the background, low classic rock drifting through the shop like it had every morning since Jonah could remember. Derek looked up when Hale entered. His expression didn't change much.

"Morning, Detective," he said calmly.

Jonah noticed something immediately. Derek didn't look surprised to see them. Hale stepped inside the shop.

"Morning."

Jonah stayed beside him. A second mechanic near the back of the bay looked between them uncertainly, sensing something in the air but not understanding it yet. Derek set the wrench down.

"What can I do for you?"

Hale didn't answer right away. He reached into his coat and removed a small evidence bag. Inside it sat the metal fuel cap. The name engraved along the underside was clearly visible. Sea Mist. Derek's eyes moved to it. For the first time since Jonah had known him, the man hesitated. Just a fraction. Then the calm expression returned.

"Looks like my boat part," Derek said.

"It is," Hale replied.

He placed the evidence bag gently on the workbench between them.

"We found it this morning."

Derek looked at the bag.

"Where?"

Hale held his gaze.

"On an island west of the crab lanes."

The words settled into the room like dust. The mechanic in the back stopped working entirely now. Jonah watched Derek carefully. The man didn't panic. Didn't argue. He simply leaned his weight slightly against the workbench and studied the evidence bag as if considering the craftsmanship of the metal.

"You're saying my boat lost a fuel cap," Derek said.

"I'm saying we found it beside a dead man."

The radio continued playing quietly somewhere behind them. Jonah could hear the faint squeak of dock lines through the open bay doors. Derek's eyes lifted slowly from the bag to Hale.

"Josh Hoggins?"

"Yes."

Another pause. Derek nodded once.

"That's unfortunate."

The words landed flat in the room. Not cruel. Not emotional. Just... practical. Jonah felt something tighten in his chest. Hale spoke again, his voice still calm.

"He died from blunt trauma. Likely several days ago."

Derek didn't look away.

"Is that right."

"We also found marsh mud inside the cabin."

Hale nodded toward the Sea Mist visible through the open doors.

"The same kind your boat deck had yesterday morning before it was washed."

Derek followed the gesture toward his boat. Then back to Hale.

"You're building a story."

"No," Hale said quietly. "I'm finishing one."

The mechanic in the back shifted uncomfortably. Derek stood up straight again.

"You're making a mistake."

Hale shook his head.

"No."

He reached for Derek's wrist.

"You're under arrest for the murder of Joshua Hoggins."

The room seemed to hold its breath. Derek didn't pull away. He simply watched the floor as Hale snapped the handcuffs into

90

place. Jonah noticed something strange then. Derek still didn't look angry. He looked... irritated. Like a man whose morning schedule had been unexpectedly interrupted.

"You'll want a lawyer," Hale said.

"Yes," Derek replied calmly.

He allowed Hale to guide him toward the door. Outside, a few dock workers had gathered quietly near the slips. Pete stood among them, his coffee mug forgotten in his hand. No one spoke.

Derek walked past them without looking at anyone. The wind moved across the harbor, carrying the faint smell of salt and engine oil. Jonah followed behind Hale as they led Derek toward the patrol car waiting near the lot. The man climbed into the back seat without resistance. Hale closed the door. For a moment he just stood there beside the vehicle.

The marina had gone almost completely silent. Jonah looked back toward the harbor. Beyond the breakwater the Pacific stretched wide and cold beneath the pale sky. Josh had been out there. Waiting. Hoping someone would come. Jonah felt the weight of it settle again. Hale spoke quietly beside him.

"You're thinking about the time."

Jonah nodded.

"We were three days late."

Hale looked out toward the water.

"Sometimes that happens."

Jonah didn't answer. Hale continued.

"The job isn't always saving people."

Jonah swallowed.

"It's finding the truth."

Hale glanced at him.

"And making sure it doesn't stay buried."

The wind moved through the marina again, rattling loose rigging against a mast somewhere behind them. Jonah looked back toward the patrol car. Inside, Derek Townsend sat quietly in the back seat staring straight ahead. No anger. No panic. Just silence. And Jonah realized something then.

For years, the town of Seabrook had lived beside that silence without questioning it. Now it had finally been broken. But it had come three days too late for Josh Hoggins. The harbor water moved slowly against the docks.

The ocean beyond continued its endless quiet breathing. And for the first time since the case began, Jonah understood something Detective Hale had tried to explain to him many times before. Finding the truth didn't always mean saving someone. Sometimes it only meant telling the story of how they were lost.

Chapter 12

The interview room at Seabrook Police Department looked exactly the way interview rooms always seemed to look in movies, except smaller and less dramatic. A metal table bolted to the floor. Three chairs.

One narrow window set high in the wall that admitted a thin wash of afternoon gray. Fluorescent lights overhead that buzzed softly and made everyone inside look a little more tired than they already were.

Jonah sat beside the wall with his hands folded loosely between his knees. Hale stood near the door for a moment before finally taking the chair across from Emily Townsend. Emily sat with both hands wrapped around a paper cup of water she had barely touched.

She looked as though the morning had taken years out of her. Not physically. Not in any obvious way. She was still neat. Still composed on the surface. Her coat was folded over the back of her chair. Her hair had been pulled back again, though more strands had come loose this time and curled near her face. But whatever careful structure she usually held herself inside had thinned. Exhausted relief. Fear not yet fully gone. And grief, already present before the words had begun.

Hale didn't rush into the silence. That was something Jonah had learned about him over the past six months. Hale understood that people often stepped toward the truth more honestly if you didn't try to drag them there too quickly.

Finally he said, "Derek's been booked."

Emily's hands tightened slightly around the paper cup. She nodded once. Not surprise. Not exactly relief either. More like a body absorbing a fact it had wanted for too long to trust immediately. Hale continued, his voice steady and quiet.

"He won't be going home tonight."

That landed differently. Jonah saw it at once. Emily's shoulders lowered, just barely. The kind of movement that might not even register to someone who didn't know what tension looked like when it had become ordinary. She looked down at the water in the cup.

"Okay," she said.

The room went quiet again. The fluorescent lights hummed overhead. Somewhere in the hallway beyond the closed door, a phone rang once, then stopped. Hale folded his hands on the table.

"We found Josh this morning."

There was no good way to say that kind of sentence. No arrangement of words that made it clean. Emily closed her eyes. Just for a second. When she opened them again, her face had gone still in a different way. Not blank. More like something inside her had finally stopped holding itself back.

"Where?" she asked.

"An island west of the crab lanes," Hale said. "In one of the seasonal cabins."

Emily looked down at the table. Jonah watched her take that in piece by piece. She had known enough to fear it. She had not known where it ended. Hale didn't soften the next part, but he didn't make it cruel either.

"He died there."

Emily's fingers tightened around the paper cup so hard the lid creased inward slightly. No tears came right away. That made it worse somehow. She sat there very still, staring at the dent her fingers had made in the thin white lid, and Jonah had the sudden sense that if anyone in the room made too much noise the whole shape of her would break apart.

Finally she whispered, "Was he alone?"

The question hit Jonah harder than anything else that had been said. Hale answered after a beat.

"Yes."

Emily nodded once. Very small. Then she covered her mouth

with one hand and looked toward the wall, away from both of them. The first tear came anyway. Not dramatic. Not sobbing. Just something that escaped despite all the careful systems she had probably lived inside for years. Jonah looked down at his hands. For a long moment no one spoke. When Emily finally lowered her hand, her voice sounded thinner than before.

"He was trying to help me."

There it was. Not as revelation. As confirmation. Hale nodded once.

"We thought so."

Emily let out something between a laugh and a breath, but there was nothing amused in it.

"Of course he was," she said quietly. "He always tried to help when he shouldn't have."

Jonah looked up. That sentence changed Josh again. Not just a rough harbor guy with bad habits. Not even just a man kind enough to care. A man who stepped into things knowing he might be stepping too far.

Hale said, "I need you to tell me about Derek."

Emily stared at the water cup. For a second Jonah wondered if she would shut down. Go silent again. Rebuild the wall she had clearly been living behind. Instead she nodded.

And when she spoke, her voice had the strange steadiness of someone who had rehearsed the truth privately for years and never believed she'd actually say it in a room where it might matter.

"He was never like that in public," she said.

Hale said nothing. Emily looked up at the high gray window.

"When I met him, everybody said the same things. Reliable. Calm. Hardworking. Respectable." She gave a faint, tired smile that vanished immediately. "They still say those things."

Jonah thought about Derek in the repair shop. Even in handcuffs he had seemed more inconvenienced than cornered. Emily continued.

"He didn't start angry. People always imagine that part wrong." She looked back down. "It started with rules. Little things. Who I talked to. Where I went. What time I got home. What I wore if we were going somewhere together."

Her thumb moved slowly over the side of the cup.

"At first it sounds like concern," she said. "That's the trick."

Hale stayed very still across from her. Emily's voice remained quiet.

"Then one day concern becomes correction. And correction becomes control. And after a while..." She swallowed lightly. "After a while you stop noticing the steps because you're too busy living inside them."

Jonah felt something in his chest tighten. Not because the words were dramatic. Because they weren't. Because she said them like weather someone had lived under so long she'd forgotten other skies existed.

Hale asked, "Did he hit you?"

Emily's face changed almost imperceptibly. Not fear. Not exactly. Recognition that the question had finally been made plain.

"Yes," she said.

The word sat in the room. Jonah stared at the table.

Hale said, "How long?"

Emily let out a breath.

"Years."

"Did anyone know?"

At that, she did smile. Faintly. Bitterly.

"People suspected."

That sentence carried everything wrong with the town inside it. The danger of silence.

The shape of a town looking away because looking all the way in would require action.

Emily's eyes moved briefly to Jonah, then back to Hale.

"They'd notice bruises. Or hear us fighting. Or notice I stopped showing up to things unless he was with me." Her voice stayed even. "But noticing and saying something aren't the same."

No one argued with that. There was nothing to argue with.

Hale asked, "When did Josh notice?"

That changed her expression again. Josh. There was grief there now, yes, but also something warmer. Sadder in a different way.

"Last fall," she said.

"Why?"

Emily looked down at the cup again.

"My car wouldn't start outside the market."

Jonah remembered what the winter docks smelled like, how the air could make engines stubborn and fingers useless.

Emily said, "Derek was supposed to come get me, but he wouldn't answer. Josh happened to be there loading bait crates for a delivery run. He looked at the engine, hit the starter twice, and said the battery connection was loose."

A tiny smile touched her mouth. Real this time, but painful.

"He fixed it with a pocket knife and half a curse."

Jonah almost smiled too, though it didn't stay long. Emily's voice softened.

"He asked if I was okay."

Hale asked, "And you told him?"

She shook her head once.

"No. Not then."

"Why him?"

That one took longer.

"Because he kept asking," she said.

Not pushy. Not invasive. Just persistent in the way kind people often are when they've already noticed more than is comfortable. Emily continued.

"He'd see me around town. At the marina. At the market. Sometimes he'd just say hi and leave it there. Sometimes he'd ask if Derek had calmed down." Her mouth tightened. "Eventually I asked how he knew Derek needed calming down."

Hale leaned back slightly, letting her keep the shape of the story.

Emily continued, "Josh told me men like Derek always think nobody can see them. But men like Josh spend their whole lives noticing which men are dangerous."

Jonah felt that sentence settle hard. Because it explained something too. Why Josh had stepped in. Why the rough edges people dismissed might have come with their own kind of knowledge.

"What happened then?" Hale asked.

Emily stared at the table.

"He offered to help me leave."

The room grew even quieter. Not because the words were louder than anything before. Because they changed the story from hidden violence into movement. A plan. Hope. The thing Derek would have been most threatened by.

Hale asked, "How?"

Emily blinked once, gathering herself.

"He knew some of the old crab cabins west of the lanes. Said one of them still had a working stove and a generator if the weather held." She looked at Hale. "The plan wasn't to stay there forever. Just long enough to get me out of town."

Jonah thought of the map. The circles. The X. Of course. Emily continued.

"Josh had a cousin near Tillamook who said I could stay there until I figured things out." Her voice wavered slightly on the last part. "He kept saying we needed one clean weekend. One gap where Derek thought I was somewhere else."

Hale asked, "The note in Josh's truck. Was that yours?"

Wait until he leaves. Light off if late. Use the side door. Emily looked down immediately.

"Yes."

The admission came with no resistance. Only exhaustion.

"I left it in the glove box of his truck when he was helping me bring groceries in one afternoon." She swallowed. "Derek had started checking my phone. Checking my email. He'd stand in the kitchen and ask who I'd talked to that day in exactly the tone people use when they're pretending it's normal."

Her voice had gone flatter now, not from indifference but from memory.

"I couldn't write much. Josh said keep it simple."

Hale nodded once.

"The side door to your house."

"Yes."

"And 'light off if late' meant what?"

Emily stared at the water in the cup.

"If the kitchen light was off when he drove by, it meant Derek was still awake."

Jonah felt cold move through him. That was how fear worked when it became architecture. It turned houses into signals. Lights into permissions. Silence into code.

Hale asked, "What was supposed to happen?"

Emily answered almost immediately, because she'd probably lived through the imagined version of it a hundred times.

"Friday night," she said. "Derek usually stayed late at the shop to finish invoices and payroll. Josh was going to take the small runabout from the far slips, come around the back road, and meet me behind the house. I'd already started hiding clothes in trash bags in the garage."

Her face tightened.

"We were going to leave before midnight."

Jonah thought about Josh's truck. The cash. The spare keys. The map folded and refolded until the paper had softened at the creases. It had all been real. Not an idea. A plan. Hale asked the question Jonah had been waiting for and dreading.

"What changed?"

Emily closed her eyes for a moment. Then she opened them and looked not at Hale, but at Jonah. Maybe because he was younger. Maybe because in him she could see the shape of what happened more clearly.

"Derek found out before Friday."

There it was.

Hale said quietly, "How?"

Emily shook her head.

"I don't know."

Then after a second: "Maybe he saw me packing. Maybe he followed Josh. Maybe he just noticed I wasn't afraid the same way anymore."

That sentence stayed in the room. Not afraid the same way

anymore. Hope had changed her. And Derek had seen it. Emily looked back to Hale.

"The day they fought at the marina, Josh came by the side yard in the morning. He said Derek had been asking strange questions. About who he talked to. About why he'd been seen near our street." Her hand trembled once against the cup. "He told me to wait. Said maybe we should move sooner."

Jonah leaned forward slightly without meaning to.

"You saw him that day?"

Emily nodded.

"Yes."

The room seemed to contract around that.

Hale asked, "When was the last time?"

Emily swallowed hard.

"Around noon."

"After the fight?"

"I don't know when the fight was."

Jonah spoke for the first time in several minutes.

"He told Calvin if Derek found out before the weekend, it was over."

Emily looked at him. Something in her face broke a little more.

"He said that?"

Jonah nodded. She looked down.

"Then he knew."

Hale asked, "Knew what?"

Emily's voice became very quiet.

"That Derek had figured it out."

For a moment none of them spoke.

Then Hale said, "Tell me about that night."

Emily's fingers loosened around the cup at last, though she didn't let go of it.

"He came home earlier than usual," she said. "Derek."

She took a breath that trembled slightly on the way in.

"He was calm."

Jonah and Hale exchanged the briefest glance. Of course he

was. Emily continued.

"He asked if I wanted dinner. Asked if I'd been anywhere that day. Told me Josh Hoggins wasn't as harmless as people thought." Her voice thinned. "He kept looking at me while he said it."

Hale let her keep going.

"I knew then," she said. "I just didn't know how much he knew."

"Did you hear from Josh?"

Emily shook her head.

"I kept waiting for him to come by. Or call from somebody else's phone. Or..." She stopped, swallowed, and tried again. "I told myself he'd gone somewhere until it blew over."

Jonah knew what that sounded like. Not stupidity. Survival. People trapped in fear often had to choose which version of reality let them remain upright for another hour.

Hale asked gently, "Did Derek ever say Josh attacked him?"

Emily looked at him with something close to disbelief.

"No."

"Did he mention the island?"

At that, she flinched slightly. So small Jonah might have missed it if he hadn't been waiting inside the room with all his attention. Hale saw it too.

"Emily."

She looked at the table.

"He said one thing," she whispered.

"What?"

"He came home late the next morning. His boots were muddy. Marsh mud. He was cleaning them in the sink and he told me..." She stopped and shook her head once, as if the sentence still had splinters in it. "He told me some men make terrible choices when they think they're rescuing someone."

The fluorescent lights hummed overhead. Jonah could hear his own breathing in the room. Hale's voice stayed careful.

"Did he threaten you?"

Emily gave a faint nod.

"Not directly."

"How, then?"

She looked at Jonah again for a brief second, then back to Hale.

"He said Seabrook was a small town and accidents had a way of becoming stories people got wrong forever." Her eyes filled again, though the tears still came slowly. "And then he asked me if I wanted to be responsible for more than one ruin."

No one in the room moved. Because that was the thing about men like Derek. They didn't always need to raise their voices when the structure of the threat was already built. Hale spoke after a long moment.

"You understand we'll need a full statement."

Emily nodded once.

"I know."

"And we'll need to put you somewhere safe tonight."

Another nod. This one came easier. Then Jonah asked the question that had been sitting in him since the island.

"Why didn't you tell anyone?"

The words came out quieter than he expected. Not accusing. Not even demanding. Just honest. Emily turned toward him fully for the first time since entering the room. He saw then how tired she truly was. Not this week. Not this month. Years.

"When people are dangerous quietly," she said, "you start to feel crazy trying to explain them out loud."

Jonah held her gaze.

Emily continued, "And once everyone around you gets used to your silence, breaking it starts to feel like the dangerous thing."

That was it. The whole truth of it. The whole town. The quiet thing everyone had been avoiding. Silence didn't just hide harm. It trained people to believe speaking was the real risk. Jonah looked down.

He thought about the harbor workers who suspected. The neighbors who probably heard fights. The way Derek moved through town like a man protected by his own steadiness. The way Josh, rough and loud and easy to dismiss, had still been the one who acted. Hale stood slowly from his chair.

"We'll get your statement recorded in a minute," he said. "Then I'll have someone take you to a motel outside town until we sort next steps."

Emily nodded, then said, "I'm leaving."

Hale paused.

"Leaving Seabrook?"

"Yes."

The answer was immediate. Firm in a way little else had been.

"There's nothing here I want to stay for," she said quietly. Then, after a beat, "Nothing that doesn't already hurt."

Jonah believed her. The town had become too full of roads she had walked under control, too many doorways she had entered measuring tone and timing and weather. Even if Derek never came home again, the shape of his presence would still sit in those places for a long time. Jonah understood that more than he realized.

Hale asked, "Where will you go?"

Emily looked down at the paper cup again.

"Anywhere that doesn't know my married name first."

That stayed with Jonah too. Not a destination. Just escape. The purest form of it. Hale left the room for a few minutes to get another officer and a recorder. That left Jonah and Emily alone. The silence between them wasn't empty. Just fragile.

Finally Emily said, "Josh talked about you."

Jonah looked up, startled.

"He did?"

She nodded.

"Not by name at first. He said there was a kid in town who noticed things other people didn't." A tired almost smile touched her mouth. "Then later he said your name."

Jonah didn't know what to do with that. Emily looked at the high gray window.

"He thought Seabrook had more people like him than people believed," she said. "People who would step in if they saw clearly enough."

Jonah swallowed.

"He stepped in."

"Yes."

The grief in that one word was sharper now. Cleaner.

"He shouldn't have had to do it alone," Emily said.

Jonah thought about the market. The bruises people probably pretended not to notice. The way silence settled over respectable men like a protective coat. No, Josh shouldn't have had to do it alone. But he had. And now that truth sat in the room with them as firmly as the table bolted to the floor. When Hale returned with the recorder and another officer, Jonah stood. Emily looked up at him one last time.

"Thank you," she said.

He didn't answer right away. Because it didn't feel like thanks fit what had happened.

Finally he said, "I'm sorry we were late."

Emily's face changed then, not with offense but with a deep sadness that seemed older than the week.

"So am I."

Jonah stepped into the hallway while Hale began the formal statement. The station felt too bright after the interview room. Phones rang. A printer hummed in the front office. Someone laughed quietly at something down the hall, then stopped as if they remembered where they were. Normal sounds. Terrible sounds. The kind the world always seemed to keep making even while someone else's life had split open in a room nearby.

Jonah stood by the window at the end of the hallway and looked out at Harbor Road. Rain had started again. Light, persistent, silvering the pavement. Seabrook moved beneath it in the same quiet way it always had. Cars passed. People crossed sidewalks with umbrellas angled against the wind. The diner's OPEN sign glowed red in its front window. Nothing in the town's shape announced what had just been said two rooms away. That felt fitting somehow. Silence had protected Derek. And now silence had to be broken piece by piece in places that looked too ordinary for the truths they held.

By the time Hale emerged an hour later, his face had that

settled tiredness Jonah had started recognizing as the aftermath of difficult truth finally put on record.

"She's done," he said.

Jonah nodded.

"She's leaving?"

"Yes."

Hale stood beside him at the window.

"We'll get her out tonight."

Jonah looked down at the rain-dark street.

"She should go."

"Yeah."

For a while they stood there without speaking.

Then Jonah said, "Josh saved her."

Hale looked at him.

"Not in the way he planned," Jonah continued. "But he did."

Hale's gaze returned to the street.

"Yes."

That didn't make it less tragic. Maybe it made it more so. Because Josh had risked himself to interrupt silence. And in the end, even in death, he had done it.

Jonah thought about the island cabin. The map. The note. The side door. The kitchen light. The whole hidden language of escape two people had built because they believed saying things aloud in Seabrook was more dangerous than speaking in code.

Then he thought about Emily's face when she said, "People are dangerous quietly." And he understood something more clearly than before. Violence did not always arrive as chaos. Sometimes it arrived as calm routines. As respected voices. As men who opened their shops on time and greeted neighbors politely and made the people around them question their own fear until silence felt easier than truth.

Hale said, "You alright?"

Jonah looked out at the rain.

"No."

Hale nodded once as if that were the correct answer.

"That makes sense."

In the parking lot below, a police sedan pulled around to the side entrance to take Emily somewhere safe for the night. Somewhere outside Seabrook. Somewhere her married name meant nothing. Jonah watched the car idle there in the rain. And for the first time since Josh Hoggins went missing, the shape of the truth settled fully inside him.

Silence had cost a man his life. Speech had come too late to save him. But not too late to keep the story from ending where Derek wanted it to. That mattered. It just didn't feel like enough.

Chapter 13

The marina felt different in the afternoon. Not louder. Not quieter. Just... altered. Jonah walked slowly along the wooden dock with his hands buried deep in his jacket pockets. The tide had come in since morning, lifting the boats higher against their moorings. Lines creaked softly against the cleats. Water tapped rhythmically against the hulls.

Above him, gulls circled the harbor in slow drifting arcs. They cried out now and then, sharp and lonely sounds that carried across the gray sky. Six months ago he would have walked through this place without noticing half of it.

Now everything felt louder to him. Not in sound. In meaning. He passed the slip where the Sea Mist had been tied earlier that morning. The space was empty now. Only the wet imprint of the hull remained against the pilings where the waterline had brushed them.

Derek Townsend was sitting in a county holding cell two towns away. The man who had run this marina like a quiet kingdom was gone. But the docks still moved with the same small rhythms. Boats shifted with the tide. Lines strained and relaxed with the wind.

Life didn't stop because truth arrived. Jonah kept walking. A few harbor workers noticed him as he passed. Pete Landry stood outside the harbor office again, though this time he wasn't holding coffee. He leaned against the railing with his arms folded, watching the water. When he saw Jonah approaching, he nodded once.

"Hell of a week," Pete said.

Jonah nodded back.

"Yeah."

Pete rubbed the back of his neck.

"They took Townsend out in cuffs this morning."

"Yeah."

Pete looked out across the harbor for a moment.

"Never liked that guy," he muttered.

Jonah didn't answer. That sentence had already started appearing around town in different forms. Never trusted him. Always thought something was off. Knew he was trouble. The strange thing about hindsight was how easily it rewrote people's memories.

Pete continued, "Whole place thought Josh just got drunk and took a boat out."

Jonah looked down the dock. Somewhere farther out, a buoy bell clanged softly against the rolling swell.

"People still saying that?" Jonah asked.

Pete shrugged.

"Some are."

That didn't surprise Jonah. Stories had momentum once they started moving. Even when the truth arrived, the old version sometimes kept drifting along beside it. Pete pushed away from the railing.

"They'll sort it out eventually."

Jonah nodded.

"Yeah."

But he wasn't sure that was true. The truth didn't always travel faster than the comfortable version. Pete looked like he wanted to say something else. Instead he gave Jonah a tired pat on the shoulder as he walked past.

"Take care of yourself, kid."

Jonah continued down the dock. The gulls wheeled overhead again. Their cries echoed across the water like something restless and searching. He passed Josh Hoggins' truck near the edge of the marina lot. It was still there. Parked crookedly beside the chain-link fence, just the way it had been the day Josh disappeared. A thin layer of salt spray had dried across the windshield.

Someone had left something on the hood. Jonah stepped

closer. A small bunch of grocery-store flowers sat there, their stems wrapped loosely in damp paper towel. Next to them lay a pack of cigarettes. Unopened. No note. Jonah stared at them for a moment.

That was how places like Seabrook mourned sometimes. Not speeches. Not memorials. Just small quiet acknowledgments left in places where people used to stand. A gull landed on the fence nearby and tilted its head, watching him. Jonah leaned against the truck bed.

He could still see Josh leaning against this same spot a week earlier, digging through his pockets for keys and complaining about the weather. Jonah remembered the way Josh had talked. The way he'd laughed. The way he'd looked over his shoulder once while they were talking, as if measuring something invisible moving through the harbor. He had known. Maybe not everything. But enough. Josh had stepped forward anyway. Jonah let out a slow breath.

"You didn't have to do it alone," he murmured quietly.

The gull on the fence flapped its wings and lifted back into the sky. Jonah watched it climb into the gray air.

A voice behind him said, "You look like you're carrying the whole harbor on your shoulders."

Jonah turned. Mara stood a few steps away. Her backpack hung loosely from one shoulder, and the wind had blown a few strands of her hair across her face. She pushed them back absent-mindedly as she walked closer.

"I heard what happened," she said.

Jonah nodded once.

"Yeah."

She looked toward the marina.

"They arrested Townsend."

"Yeah."

Mara slipped her hands into the pockets of her coat. The two of them stood quietly for a moment.

Finally she said, "People at school are saying a lot of things."

Jonah smiled faintly.

"I can imagine."

"Some still think Josh just fell off a boat."

Jonah nodded.

"Yeah."

Mara studied his face carefully.

"You were there when they arrested him, weren't you?"

Jonah hesitated. Then he nodded.

"Yeah."

"Was he...?"

She trailed off. Jonah understood the question.

"No," he said.

"No what?"

"No yelling. No fight. Nothing like that."

Mara tilted her head slightly.

"Then what?"

Jonah looked out toward the open water beyond the harbor.

"He just stood there," he said. "Like it was another normal day."

Mara frowned.

"That's... strange."

Jonah nodded slowly.

"Yeah."

Above them, the gulls circled again.

Mara followed his gaze.

"You ever notice how those birds never leave?" she said.

Jonah glanced up.

"They go wherever the boats go."

"Exactly."

She watched them for a moment.

"They're always here."

Jonah nodded. The harbor stretched quietly before them. Boats rocked gently in their slips. A fisherman farther down the dock untangled a net while humming something under his breath. Everything looked ordinary. But Jonah knew better now.

He had learned something over the past six months. Places didn't reveal their truth all at once. You had to notice the small things. The pauses. The looks people gave each other when certain names came up. The silence where questions should have been. Mara spoke again.

"You found him, didn't you?"

Jonah didn't answer right away.

Finally he said, "Yeah."

She studied his face.

"Was it bad?"

Jonah looked down at the dock boards. The grain of the wood was darkened by years of salt and rain.

"Yeah," he said quietly.

Mara stepped closer.

"You okay?"

Jonah thought about the island. The cabin. The water bottle on the table. The map in Josh's truck.

"No," he said.

Mara nodded slowly.

"That makes sense."

She leaned beside him against the truck. For a while they just watched the harbor. A gull landed briefly on the railing of a nearby dock post, then launched itself back into the wind. Jonah spoke quietly.

"He tried to help someone."

Mara nodded.

"I heard."

"He almost got her out."

The wind moved through the marina again.

Mara said softly, "But he didn't."

Jonah shook his head.

"No."

They stood there together as the tide shifted slowly beneath the docks. Jonah realized something then. Seabrook felt smaller now. Not physically. Emotionally. He had grown up believing this town contained everything important in the world. But over the past six months he had started seeing its edges. The way silence moved through it. The way people looked away from things that felt uncomfortable to name. The way truths sometimes stayed buried until someone dug them out. And sometimes that digging came too late. Mara nudged his shoulder gently.

"What are you thinking about?"

Jonah watched the gulls circling high above the harbor.

"I'm thinking this place might not be where my story ends."

Mara raised an eyebrow.

"Planning on leaving already?"

Jonah shrugged slightly.

"Not yet."

But the idea had begun forming somewhere inside him. A quiet possibility. Like a path that hadn't existed before but now stretched faintly toward the horizon. One day he might need to follow it. Above them, the gulls continued their endless circling over the gray water.

Jonah Harris stood on the marina dock realizing that Seabrook, quiet, beautiful, secretive Seabrook, was no longer the whole world. Just the place where he had begun learning how to see it.

Chapter 14

The path up to Hale's bluff house always felt steeper after dark. Not physically. Jonah knew every bend in it by now. The split rail fence near the lower turn, the patch of slick stone halfway up where the rainwater always collected, the wind-bent grass along the shoulder that hissed softly when the weather shifted. But evenings changed the path.

By late day the coast liked to remind people how small they were. The sky had begun its slow descent into evening when Jonah started up from the truck. The sun was somewhere west of the clouds, not visible exactly, but its fading light had turned the horizon into long bands of silver and pale orange. Below the bluff, the Pacific rolled in heavy slate-colored lines toward the cliffs, each wave breaking with a low concussion that rose through the air and into the ground under his feet.

A gull passed overhead, crying once before the wind took the sound and stretched it thin. Jonah kept walking. The marina still sat inside him. Josh's truck. The flowers on the hood. Pete saying the harbor would sort itself out eventually. Mara standing beside him on the dock while gulls circled above the water. And beneath all of it, the same weight that had settled in him since the island. Too late. The phrase had become its own kind of tide.

He reached the last stretch of the path just as the bluff house came fully into view, its windows reflecting the dimming sky. The porch light was on. So was the lamp in the front room. Hale sat on the back porch facing the ocean with a mug in one hand and his jacket folded over the chair beside him, as if the cold belonged to the house and he had simply agreed to share the evening with it. Jonah stepped onto the porch without speaking. Hale glanced back once, then looked toward the water again.

"You eat?"

Jonah shook his head.

"Not hungry."

"That answer usually means you should've eaten."

Jonah leaned against the porch railing. Below them, the waves crashed against the rocks in hollow bursts of white that glowed faintly in the last light. Farther south, the lighthouse beam had not yet fully brightened, but its glass tower was already visible as a dim vertical shape beyond the headland.

For a minute neither of them said anything. The wind moved through the coastal grass around the bluff with a dry whisper. Somewhere farther down the slope, another gull called out and then went quiet. Hale took a sip from the mug.

"You walked the marina."

It wasn't a question. Jonah nodded once.

"Yeah."

"How was it?"

Jonah thought about that. The answer wanted to come out as a dozen small things instead of one.

"It looked normal," he said finally.

Hale nodded. "That's the problem with places. They keep looking like themselves."

Jonah looked down at the rocks below where another wave burst and pulled itself apart across the black stone.

"Pete said people will sort it out eventually."

"Maybe."

"They won't."

Hale glanced at him then, but only briefly.

"You sound sure."

Jonah shoved his hands into his pockets.

"Some of them already changed the story in their heads. Now they'll say they always knew Derek was off. Or that Josh brought trouble on himself. Or both."

The wind shifted, colder now that the sun had sunk lower behind the clouds. Hale didn't interrupt. Jonah kept going.

"It's like they need things to stay simple even after they stop being simple."

Hale set the mug down on the porch rail.

"Most people do."

Jonah looked over.

"That doesn't bother you?"

"It bothers me all the time," Hale said.

He leaned back slightly in the chair and looked out over the ocean again.

"The trick is figuring out what to do with the fact that it bothers you."

The lighthouse beam flickered on in the distance then, faint at first, then brighter as the sky dimmed another shade. Its rotation swept slowly across the water, disappeared, then returned. Jonah watched it for a second.

Then he said, "We were too late."

Hale didn't say anything right away. The ocean below kept moving, patient and indifferent.

Finally he said, "Yeah."

That helped more than Jonah expected. Not because it fixed anything. Because it wasn't denial. Not comfort. Just truth. Jonah rested his forearms on the railing.

"Three days," he said quietly. "Maybe more."

Hale nodded.

"Probably."

Jonah stared out at the water.

"If we'd seen it sooner. If we'd gone out there earlier. If.."

He didn't finish the sentence. He didn't need to. The unfinished part sat between them anyway, heavy and familiar.

If I'd noticed faster.

If I'd pushed harder.

If I'd known which clue mattered first.

Hale spoke into the silence.

"You know what the worst part of this job is?"

Jonah looked at him. The older man's face was turned toward the horizon now, his features softened and darkened by the fading light.

"It's not the bodies," Hale said. "Not really. It's the timeline."

Jonah waited.

"Once you know what happened," Hale continued, "your brain starts rearranging everything backward. You start seeing all the doors where maybe, just maybe, you could've arrived on the other side of them in time."

The words settled slowly. Jonah thought about the coffee shop. Emily's face. The note in the truck. The fog lifting over the islands. Hale went on.

"That part doesn't go away just because you know you did the best you could with what you had."

Jonah looked down.

"Did you ever get used to it?"

Hale let out a quiet breath through his nose, not quite a laugh. "No."

He picked up the mug again but didn't drink from it.

"A long time ago," he said, "before I made detective, there was a case south of Astoria. Domestic call history. Neighbors heard fighting for months. Patrol had been out there twice. Nothing visible. Nothing either of them would put on paper."

The wind moved across the bluff again, flattening the grass in one direction before letting it rise. Hale's voice stayed level.

"One night the wife managed to run. Half a mile through the woods in freezing rain. Barefoot. Deputies found her on the shoulder of the road." He paused. "Her son didn't make it out."

Jonah went still. Hale looked not at him, but at the water.

"He was nine."

The lighthouse beam crossed the ocean and vanished again.

Jonah said quietly, "Did they catch him?"

"Yes."

"That help?"

Hale took a sip from the mug at last.

"It helped her."

He set the mug down again.

"It didn't help the boy."

The sentence stayed there. No decoration. No lesson attached to it yet. Just the hard shape of a truth too old to argue with. Jonah looked out at the horizon where the last color had nearly gone from the sky.

"What did you do with that?"

Hale's expression didn't change much, but something in it deepened.

"You keep going," he said. "Not because that answer feels good. Because the alternative is letting the people who do these things own the ending."

Jonah thought about Derek in handcuffs, still calm. Still quiet. And Josh in the cabin. And Emily in the interview room saying, once everyone around you gets used to your silence, breaking it starts to feel like the dangerous thing. Hale folded one hand around the mug.

"You care too much to do this work without it hurting," he said.

Jonah glanced at him.

"That supposed to make me feel better?"

"No."

Hale's mouth moved slightly at one corner.

"It's supposed to make you stop thinking the pain means you're unsuited for it."

That landed harder than Jonah expected. Because he had been thinking that. Not in a clean sentence. More like a shadow behind several thoughts.

Maybe somebody better at this would've seen it sooner.

Maybe somebody less shaken by it would know what to do next.

Maybe people who solve things aren't supposed to carry them this way afterward.

Jonah looked down at his hands where they rested on the railing.

"What if I'm not built right for it?"

Hale answered immediately.

"You're built exactly right for it."

Jonah looked over. Hale shook his head once before he could

say anything.

"No, not because you're clever. Lots of clever people make terrible investigators. And not because you notice things. That helps, but it's not enough either."

The wind caught the lighthouse beam again, scattering it briefly over the low cloud base before it swung back across the water.

"What matters," Hale said, "is that you haven't mistaken solving something for owning it."

Jonah frowned slightly. Hale continued.

"There's a difference between finding truth and treating other people's pain like a puzzle you get credit for finishing." His voice stayed calm. "You never did that. Even when you were too curious for your own good."

Jonah almost smiled at that, but it didn't last. The ocean below them surged harder against the cliffs. Spray caught what little light remained and vanished.

Hale added, "You still see the people first."

Jonah looked back toward the horizon.

"And that's useful?"

"It's essential."

For a while neither of them spoke. The blue hour settled fully over the coast now, draining the remaining warmth from the sky. The lighthouse beam grew brighter with the darkness. Far below, the wave breaks turned from white to ghostly silver against the black rock. A gull crossed in front of the porch, wings angled against the wind, and disappeared into the dim.

Jonah said, "Emily's leaving."

Hale nodded.

"Yeah."

"She should."

"Yes."

Jonah watched the beam turn again.

"Josh was the only one who stepped in."

Hale leaned back slightly in his chair.

"He was the one who stepped in first."

Jonah looked at him.

"That matter?"

"It does."

"How?"

Hale folded his hands loosely over the mug.

"Because towns like Seabrook survive on the myth that someone else will say something if something is truly wrong." He looked out over the water. "Josh proved that myth wrong."

Jonah let that sink in. Silence protects abusers. The truth had settled into the bones of the town, where silence had once lived. Hale spoke again, quieter now.

"Sometimes all it takes for people to keep quiet is the belief that intervention belongs to someone more qualified."

Jonah thought about neighbors. Harbor workers. People at the market. The quiet collective permission of not being the first person to make a hard thing public.

He said, "And then nobody does."

"Right."

The porch light behind them clicked on automatically as the darkness deepened. Warm yellow spilled across the weathered boards and the back of Hale's chair. Jonah looked down toward the shoreline path barely visible below the bluff.

"Seabrook feels smaller now."

Hale nodded.

"That happens."

"Did that happen to you?"

A small smile crossed Hale's face then, tired and brief.

"I grew up in one town, worked in five, and disappointed two county sheriffs before lunch at least once. So yes. Places get smaller when you learn their limits."

Jonah considered that. The wind moved harder for a second, making the porch boards creak. He looked out toward the ocean.

"What happens when you learn yours?"

Hale was quiet a moment.

Then he said, "You leave before they become walls."

That sentence stayed with Jonah. Not because it told him to

go anywhere. Because it named something he had been feeling without wanting to shape into words. Seabrook no longer felt like the whole world. Just the beginning of one. Not today. Not tomorrow. But someday.

The thought didn't scare him the way it might have once. It felt... directional. Like standing in cold wind and realizing the map extends past the edge of the page you've been staring at. Hale stood and pulled on his jacket at last.

"Come on," he said. "I made chili."

Jonah glanced at him.

"That's an aggressive transition."

"It's called caretaking. Don't ruin it."

That got an actual small laugh out of Jonah. He pushed off the railing and followed Hale toward the door. Then he stopped once more and looked back at the ocean. The lighthouse beam swept over the water again. Gulls drifted as dark moving shapes against the last dim band of sky. Below, the waves kept coming in, one after another, patient as truth. Hale paused at the door.

"You coming?"

Jonah nodded.

"Yeah."

He took one last look at the coastline. At the town somewhere south beyond the headland. At the dark water stretching west into distances Seabrook had never been big enough to contain. And though he did not say it aloud, Jonah felt something settle in him with a new kind of steadiness. This town had taught him how to notice. One day, something beyond it would teach him what to do next.

Chapter 15

The gathering at the marina began without anyone saying it had. That felt right. By late afternoon the rain had thinned to a cold mist that drifted in from the harbor and settled over everything in a fine gray layer. The sky hung low over Seabrook, the color of weathered steel, and the water inside the marina moved in slow dark swells beneath the docks. Boats rocked gently in their slips. Lines creaked. A gull stood hunched on the roof of the harbor office like it had claimed the whole season as its own.

Jonah arrived with Mara. Neither of them had spoken much on the walk down Harbor Road. They didn't need to. The town itself seemed quieter than usual, as if even Seabrook understood what the afternoon was for.

Near the fuel dock, a small cluster of people stood facing the water. Pete Landry was there, hands folded over the top of a knit cap he had taken off despite the cold. Two fishermen Jonah recognized from the charter slips stood a few feet away in heavy jackets, boots damp from the weather. Eli was there too, quieter than Jonah had ever seen him. Calvin Rudd stood off to one side near a piling with his hands in his pockets and his shoulders set in a way that made him look broader than usual, not because he was trying to but because he seemed to have nowhere useful to put the weight he was carrying.

A few others from town stood farther back near the lot. People who probably knew Josh only in passing. People who had worked beside him. People who had heard the story late and come anyway.

No one had set up chairs. No flowers were arranged in neat bundles. No church words or official program waited in anyone's hands. The gathering simply existed because enough people had shown up and chosen not to leave.

Hale stood near the edge of the dock, not with the group exactly and not apart from it either. His hands were in his coat pockets, his expression unreadable in the damp air. When Jonah and Mara reached the dock, Hale looked at them once and gave a small nod. That was all.

Jonah and Mara stepped into the quiet without speaking. The harbor beyond the slips stretched toward the breakwater in bands of dark water and pale mist. Out past that, the Pacific breathed in heavy slow swells beneath the gray sky. Somewhere beyond sight, the island waited under the same weather, its small cabin empty now except for evidence markers and silence.

Pete cleared his throat softly. It was not a speech. More like a man making sure his voice still worked before he trusted it with something important.

"Josh was a pain in the neck," Pete said.

That got the faintest broken laugh out of Eli and one of the older fishermen. Pete looked down at the knit cap in his hands.

"He was late half the time. Borrowed things he didn't return. Returned things he did borrow and acted like that was some kind of personal favor to the rest of us." He paused. "But he showed up when people needed him. Even when they didn't deserve it."

The wind moved across the dock. Pete lifted his eyes toward the water.

"Seems worth saying out loud."

No one answered immediately. They didn't need to. Calvin was the one who spoke next, which surprised Jonah. The man kept his gaze on the harbor and spoke so quietly Jonah almost missed the first words.

"I owe him fifty bucks."

A few heads turned.

Calvin shrugged without looking at anyone.

"He fixed the starter on my brother's skiff in October and told me to pay him later. I forgot. He didn't."

That got another brief, tired almost-laugh from somewhere near the back. Calvin's mouth moved once at one corner, but it never became a smile.

"He was a mess," he said. "But he wasn't a coward."

The sentence landed hard and clean. Jonah looked out at the water. Not a coward. No. Josh Hoggins had seen something wrong and stepped toward it anyway. Roughly. Imperfectly. Without the right plan, maybe. But with more courage than most people in Seabrook had found in themselves while standing comfortably on shore.

Pete reached down beside the piling and picked up a small cardboard box. Inside were white flowers. Nothing expensive. Just grocery-store stems wrapped loosely in paper towels to keep them from freezing too hard in the mist. The same kind of flowers Jonah had seen on Josh's truck, only more of them now.

Pete held the box out first to the men nearest him. No instructions. No announcement. One by one, people took a few flowers and stepped closer to the railing. Jonah took two when the box reached him. Mara took one and stood beside him with her coat drawn tight at the neck. The dock had gone very still now. Even the gulls overhead seemed quieter, their circling lower and slower above the slips.

Pete was the first to throw his flowers. He didn't make a gesture of it. He simply let them go. White blossoms fell through the damp air and struck the water with almost no sound at all before beginning to drift outward on the tide.

After that, the others followed. Flowers touched the harbor and spread apart slowly across the dark surface. A few petals broke loose at once and floated away on their own, small pale shapes carried between the slips toward the channel.

Mara released hers next. Then Jonah let his go. The white flowers spun once in the water and began drifting with the others.

Above them, the gulls broke their lazy circles and scattered suddenly, lifting into the mist in a burst of white wings as if the motion below had startled them. Their cries echoed briefly across the harbor before fading into the gray.

Jonah watched the flowers move. The tide caught them in slow pieces, drawing them farther out between the pilings. They looked almost unreal against the dark water. Too delicate for a place like this. Too soft for the hard edges of the marina. But that seemed right too.

Josh Hoggins had not been soft. He had been loud, difficult, messy, and not nearly as invisible as people pretended. But the truth about him had required a gentler shape than the reputation Seabrook had given him. A man can be reckless and still brave. Difficult and still kind. Broken around the edges and still the first one willing to step forward.

The flowers drifted farther toward the harbor mouth. One of the older fishermen removed his cap. The others followed. No one said anything for nearly a full minute. No speeches. No prayer.

Just the wind, the tide, and the creak of boats rocking gently against their lines. Jonah looked back once toward the marina lot. Josh's truck was still there. The flowers someone had left on the hood earlier had grown damp and bent under the mist. The whole truck looked like a sentence no one had finished.

Near the repair slips, Townsend Marine stood dark and closed. The bay doors were shut now. The sign over the building looked smaller without work lights beneath it. Someone had taped brown paper over the office windows from the inside. The Sea Mist was gone too, taken for processing. In their absence, the place looked less like a business and more like an outline of authority that had lost the man who held it together. A few people at the back of the gathering murmured quietly to each other. Jonah caught pieces as the wind shifted.

"...always thought something was off..."

"...no, I'm telling you, he probably hit Josh at the dock..."

"...they still said the first day he'd gone out drinking..."

"...that's not what happened..."

The old story and the new truth moving alongside each other. The town correcting itself, but not all at once. Never all at once. Some people would still repeat the drunk-boat version for weeks because it was simple and familiar and didn't require them to examine why a respectable man could hide violence so easily in plain sight.

Others had already begun reshaping Josh into a different kind of story. A better one. Maybe even too clean. That was the risk after death too. A rough life sanded smooth into memory because the dead no longer got to object.

Truth was harder than either version. Josh had been what he was. And he had still stepped forward when others didn't. The gathering ended the way it began. Quietly.

No one dismissed anyone. People simply began drifting apart in twos and threes, hats pulled back on, collars turned up against the damp air. Pete returned the empty cardboard box to the harbor office without ceremony. Eli stood with Calvin a moment longer than Jonah would have expected, then both men went their separate ways.

Hale remained near the edge of the dock, hands still in his pockets. Mara stood close enough beside Jonah that their coat sleeves brushed when the wind moved.

"You okay?" she asked softly.

Jonah looked out at the flowers still drifting between the slips. "No," he said.

Mara nodded. That seemed to be enough. She followed his gaze toward the water.

"People are still whispering about the boat thing," she said.

"Yeah."

"They will for a while."

"Yeah."

Her voice stayed low.

"But not forever."

Jonah wasn't sure about that. Some stories lingered because they were wrong in ways people found easier to live beside than the truth. And sometimes even when the facts changed, the feeling attached to the first story remained, stubborn as barnacles on a piling.

He said, "It took a dead man and an island cabin for people to stop looking away."

Mara looked at him.

"Some of them are probably still looking away."

That was true too. The gulls returned overhead one by one, slower this time, drifting on the wind above the harbor as if the brief burst of motion had resolved whatever argument they'd been having with the weather. Mara tucked a loose strand of hair behind her ear.

"You don't have to stay here all evening."

Jonah looked at the water again.

"I know."

But he stayed where he was until Hale finally came over. The detective didn't say much. He just rested one hand lightly on Jonah's shoulder for a second, then moved on toward the harbor office to speak with Pete. That was enough too. Mara stood beside Jonah another minute.

Then she said, "I've got to head back."

He nodded. She looked like she wanted to say something else. Instead she just gave him a small, searching look that held more understanding than most people managed with full conversations.

"I'll see you," she said.

"Yeah."

Then she turned and walked up the dock toward the lot, her shape gradually softening into mist and distance until she disappeared among the parked trucks and the weather-gray afternoon. Jonah remained.

The harbor had thinned now. Only the ordinary workers still moved among the slips, returning to rope and gear and engines and all the practical things the living always had to keep doing. He started walking. Not toward the lot. Toward the far end of the marina where the outer docks narrowed and the noise of the harbor thinned into water, wind, and the occasional cry of gulls overhead.

The boards under his boots were slick from mist. His hands stayed in his coat pockets. The flowers on the water had almost reached the channel now, breaking apart into smaller drifting clusters as the tide carried them between pilings and into open water.

Jonah walked past the last fuel dock and toward the outer

slips where the view widened. Out there, the breakwater markers stood dark against the gray sea. Beyond them the Pacific stretched westward in long muted bands, and somewhere beneath that low horizon sat the island where Josh had died. Jonah stopped at the end of the dock. The cold wind hit harder there. A gull landed on a post a few feet away and looked at him with one bright indifferent eye. He looked back out toward the open water.

Josh's courage. The town's silence. The weight of truth. And the quiet steady realization that Seabrook might not be where he belonged forever. All of it sat together now. Not neatly. But honestly.

He thought about the night everything in his life had first broken open. The quarry. The truth about his father. His mother being taken away in the back of a patrol car.

For a long time, he had believed that once those secrets were uncovered, Seabrook might finally feel clean again. Instead, the town had only grown more complicated. More human. More limited.

Then Josh Hoggins had disappeared, and Seabrook had shown him something else. A town could be beautiful and quiet and still teach its people how to remain silent around the wrong things. A town could hold memory and safety and still not be enough.

The gull on the piling lifted off again, wings catching the wind, and sailed outward toward the channel. Jonah followed its path with his eyes until it disappeared into the gray. Then he turned and began walking slowly back down the dock.

Behind him, the harbor continued its small ordinary sounds. Ahead of him, the marina lot waited in mist and dim afternoon light. Somewhere beyond that, Harbor Road climbed back toward town. Somewhere beyond town, the bluff house overlooked the ocean. And somewhere even farther beyond all of it, unseen for now, stretched a future that Seabrook had only begun to point him toward.

When he reached the midpoint of the dock, Jonah looked once more toward the islands. Then he kept walking. Because whatever came next, he understood now that staying in one place too long could become its own kind of silence. And he wasn't sure he could live with that.

Chapter 16

The dock was nearly empty by the time Jonah reached it. Night had settled over Seabrook in quiet layers. The last of the gray had left the sky, replaced by a deep coastal blue that turned almost black over the water. Harbor lights glowed in the distance, small yellow reflections trembling on the surface. Farther out, beyond the breakwater, the Pacific moved in darkness, its shape visible only in the rhythm of the tide and the dull white line of waves breaking against rock.

Jonah walked to the end of the dock and stopped. The wood beneath his boots was cold and faintly damp. It held the smell of salt, old rope, and years of weather. A gull cried somewhere overhead, then another answered from farther inland, the sound thin and lonely in the dark.

He rested his hands on the railing and looked out toward the channel. The tide was moving out. He could feel it in the slow pull of the water beneath the boards. The harbor no longer felt still. It felt like something in motion, subtle but undeniable, carrying whatever floated on its surface toward the open water beyond town.

Somewhere out there, too far to see now, lay the island. The cabin. The place where Josh Hoggins had died alone after trying to help someone escape. Jonah had thought about him all day.

Not the version of Josh the town had always carried around so casually, the loud one, the unreliable one, the guy people rolled their eyes at and expected trouble from. That version had been real, too. But it had not been the whole of him.

Now the rest was real too. Josh, standing near a broken car outside the market, fixing a battery connection with a pocket knife and half a curse. Josh noticing something wrong because men like him had spent their lives noticing which other men were dangerous. Josh stepping in when other people stayed silent. Jonah looked down at the black water beneath the dock.

A person could be messy and still brave. A person could be hard to like and still do the right thing. A person could carry a bad reputation through town and still end up being the one who tried to save somebody.

The tide moved under the boards with a slow hollow sound. Jonah looked toward the lighthouse in the distance. The beam swept once across the water, disappeared, then returned again, cutting a pale path through the dark before moving on.

He heard footsteps behind him. He didn't turn right away. The steps were light. Familiar. Careful in the way someone walked on old wood when they knew where the uneven boards were.

"Thought you might be here."

Jonah looked back. Mara stood a few feet away with her hands tucked into the pockets of her coat. The wind had loosened strands of her hair again, and the dock light behind her caught the edges of them in pale gold. She looked cold but not surprised to find him. Jonah gave a small nod.

"Yeah."

She walked down the last few feet of dock and stopped beside him at the railing. For a while neither of them spoke. The silence between them wasn't uncomfortable. It never had been. That was part of what made Mara different from everyone else. She didn't rush to fill quiet with words just because quiet existed. Below them, the tide kept moving out. Mara looked toward the harbor lights.

"I almost went to the marina first," she said. "Then I figured if you were thinking too much, you'd pick somewhere darker and colder."

Jonah almost smiled.

"That seems unfair."

"It's not unfair if it's true."

He let out a quiet breath through his nose. Maybe that counted as a laugh. Maybe not. The lighthouse beam swept across the water again. Mara followed it with her eyes.

"How are you doing?"

Jonah looked back toward the channel. That was a question people had asked him a lot lately, and most of the time they didn't really mean it. They meant: are you stable enough to let me stop worrying for now? Mara actually meant the question. So he answered honestly.

"I don't know."

She nodded.

"That sounds right."

The gulls cried again somewhere above the harbor. Their shapes were only shadows now, moving against a darker sky. Mara rested her forearms on the railing.

"I keep thinking about Emily," she said quietly.

Jonah nodded.

"Yeah."

"She's really leaving?"

"Tonight or tomorrow, I think."

Mara looked down at the water.

"Good."

It wasn't said harshly. Not good because the whole thing was over. Good because leaving was the first honest thing the town had allowed her in a long time. Jonah thought about Emily saying there was nothing in Seabrook she wanted to stay for that didn't already hurt. He could understand that. Mara glanced at him.

"You keep doing that face."

"What face?"

"The one where you stare at the ocean like it owes you answers."

Jonah looked back out at the dark water.

"Maybe it does."

Mara made a small sound that might have been agreement. The tide pulled harder now, a steady outward motion beneath the dock. In the distance, near the marina mouth, something pale drifted slowly through the channel. Jonah narrowed his eyes.

At first it looked like scraps of light on the water. Then he realized what they were. The flowers. Or what was left of them. The white blossoms the harbor workers had tossed into the water that afternoon had broken apart into scattered petals and small drifting clusters. Now the tide was carrying them outward, past the slips, toward the breakwater and whatever waited beyond it. Mara saw them too.

"They made it this far."

Jonah nodded.

"Yeah."

They watched the petals drift for a while. The harbor had broken them up, but the tide had not taken them under. Not yet. Mara spoke again, softer now.

"You know, for a while everyone was saying they weren't suprised Josh went missing."

Jonah's jaw tightened slightly.

"Some probably still aren't."

"Yeah."

She looked at the petals again.

"But that's not his story now."

No. Not anymore. Now the story belonged to a man who had noticed something wrong and stepped toward it. A man who had tried to help someone leave. A man who died because a quiet kind of violence had gone unchallenged too long.

Jonah said, "He shouldn't have had to do it alone."

Mara looked at him.

"No."

They stood in silence again. Then Mara asked the question that had probably been there all along.

"What happens now?"

Jonah knew she meant more than the case. Derek would go to trial. Emily would leave. The town would talk. The marina would keep working. The repair shop would sit dark for a while until someone figured out what to do with it. But that wasn't what she was really asking. He looked out toward the horizon where the ocean disappeared into night.

"I think..." He stopped, searching for the shape of it. "I think I stay here for now."

Mara nodded once, waiting.

"But?"

Jonah almost smiled without meaning to.

"You always know when there's a but."

"You always say one with your face first."

That was probably true. He looked back toward the lighthouse as the beam swept the water again.

"Seabrook taught me how to see things," he said quietly. "I just don't think it's the only place I'm supposed to look."

The words hung between them in the cold air. Not dramatic. Not a declaration. Just a truth that had finally become clear enough to say aloud. Mara turned her head and studied him for a moment.

"You're talking about leaving."

"Someday."

"Not now."

"No."

The answer came easily. That mattered. He wasn't running. He wasn't escaping. He was simply beginning to understand that towns, like people, could become too small for the person you were turning into. Mara looked back out at the water.

"For what it's worth," she said, "I've kind of suspected that for a while."

Jonah glanced at her.

"What gave it away?"

She tilted her head slightly.

"You notice things nobody else does. Then you actually do something with it." A faint smile touched one corner of her mouth. "Places like Seabrook usually don't know what to do with people like that."

Jonah thought about Derek. The quarry. His father. Josh. Emily.

"No," he said. "They usually don't."

Mara tucked her chin a little deeper into the collar of her coat against the wind.

"Then I guess wherever you go next…" She shrugged lightly. "Someone's going to need you there too."

The sentence landed softly. No accusation. No sadness sharpened into guilt. Just trust. Jonah looked at her for a long moment.

Then he said, "You make that sound simple."

"It's not simple."

"What is it, then?"

Mara looked out toward the channel where the last flowers drifted closer to open water.

"It's just true."

The lighthouse beam crossed over them briefly, silvering the railing and the edges of Mara's coat before moving on into the dark. Below, the tide kept carrying the harbor outward.

Jonah thought about Hale on the porch saying places get smaller when you learn their limits. He thought about Emily leaving because staying had become its own kind of wound. He thought about Josh, who had seen danger clearly and stepped in anyway. And he thought about the quiet steady realization that had been growing in him for months now, first with the quarry, then with the harbor, then with all the spaces in town where silence had tried to pass as peace.

Seabrook was where he had learned to notice. Where he had learned that truth could hide inside respectable faces and quiet routines. Where he had learned that solving something did not always mean saving someone. And maybe, someday, that would mean he had to leave. Not because the town had nothing left to give him. Because it had already given him the first thing he needed.

The gulls wheeled overhead again, their cries carried thin across the dark water. Mara stood beside him in the cold without asking him to become lighter than he was. The final petals drifted through the mouth of the harbor and disappeared into the black pull of the tide beyond the breakwater. And Jonah watched them go.